MW00829967

Death By Bourbon

A Josiah Reynolds Mystery

Abigail Keam

Worker Bee Press

Abigail Keam

Death By Bourbon
Copyright © Abigail Keam 2012

ALL RIGHTS RESERVED

No part of this book may be reproduced or transmitted in
any form without written permission of the author.

ISBN 978 0 615 65159 0

All characters are fictional and similarity to any living person
is just coincidence unless stated otherwise.
It's not you. So don't go around town and brag about it.

The historical facts about Kentucky are true.
The geography is true. The beekeeping is true.
The artists are real, but the art may not be.

For more information on the historical stories presented in this book – read
The Frontiersmen by Allan W. Eckert
A History of Kentucky by Thomas D.Clark Ph.D.
Both men are legends as historians and unprecedented writers.

Worker Bee Press
P.O. Box 485
Nicholasville, KY 40340

Acknowledgements

The author wishes to thank Al's Bar, which consented to be used as a drinking hole for my poetry-writing cop, Kelly, and Morris Book Shop. www.morrisbookshop.com.

Thanks to my editor, Patti De Young.

Thanks to the Lexington Farmers' Market, which has given me a home for many years. www.lexingtonfarmersmarket.com

Artwork by Cricket Press www.cricket-press.com

Book jacket by Peter Keam Author's photograph by Peter Keam

Abigail Keam

By The Same Author

Death By A HoneyBee
2010
Readers' Favorite Gold Medal Award 2010
Finalist of USA Book News Best Books of 2011

Death By Drowning
2011
Readers' Favorite Gold Medal Award 2011
Finalist of USA Book News Best Books of 2011

Death By Bridle
2012

Death By Lotto
2013

To Melanie, Sally, Anna, Bunny, Debbie, Sarah, Phil, Willie and Judith – friends who go out of their way to support my writing.

Abigail Keam

THE NIGHT BRANNON LEFT

Asa was home from Washington, licking her wounds. Her trial by fire was over and the lawyers had been paid due to the fact that I had remortgaged the Butterfly. Brannon and I were in debt again. Big debt.

I was hoping that he would be home early so we could discuss how to negotiate our way back to financial solvency. I had gone to the bank today to cash a check and discovered that thousands were missing from our household account. Brannon needed to tell me where he had mislaid his paychecks so I could put them in the bank.

Brannon was getting so absent-minded lately. He rarely spoke anymore and seemed to be brooding about something. I was wondering if his architectural firm was having trouble.

"I hear Dad's car," said Asa, setting the Nakashima table.

Looking up from the stove, I checked the kitchen clock. "He's on time tonight."

Pulling the pot roast from the oven, I poured it and steaming vegetables into a big bowl. Tasting its juices, I purred, "Just right. Hope this puts your father in a good mood."

"What's up with that?" asked Asa, fearful that her troubles were causing a breach between she and her father.

He didn't even seem to care about what she had been through the past year. He never spoke of it or gave her any encouragement. She wondered if he blamed her for the controversy.

Shaking my head, I replied, "Don't know, baby, but I've got to talk to him about our finances. I don't have enough in the household account to pay the bills."

"Well, something's going on," she concurred.

Before she could continue, Brannon came in through the front door and popped his head into the kitchen.

"Hey," he said.

"Hey to you," I returned. "Dinner is ready."

"Great," Brannon replied. "I'm going to freshen up. Be just a minute."

"No problem."

I put the food on the table. After washing our hands, Asa and I took our places at my beloved Nakashima table where we waited and waited and waited.

Asa started to rise when I motioned for her to sit back down.

Concerned, I folded my napkin and went into the bedroom. The bathroom door was shut.

Knocking on it, I asked, "Brannon, are you all right? Dinner's getting cold."

"Be right there," he called through the door. "Just go on and start."

If I had been smart, I would have looked around the room but I didn't. I just went back to the dining room. "He says to go ahead," I relayed to Asa.

Asa picked up a roll while I spooned some veggies and a big slice of roast beef onto Brannon's plate. I then filled her plate and mine.

Brannon strolled in and took his place at the table.

"How was work today, Dad?" asked Asa.

"Fine, fine," he mumbled while biting into a slice of roast. "Very good," he said to me. "Always was partial to your pot roast, dear."

I gave Brannon a big smile.

We chitchatted about little things. I told him that I had seen the pileated woodpeckers today, a rare sight in Central Kentucky, and that I had decided to teach a summer course.

"Why's that?" he asked.

"We could use the money," I said matter of factly. "Speaking of money, I went to the bank today to cash a check and the household account is missing quite a bit. Did you forget to cash your paychecks?"

Brannon swallowed his food and was quiet for a moment. "Can we talk about this after dinner? I hate being interrogated when I'm trying to eat."

Stunned, I answered, "Of course. I was just asking. I didn't mean to come off that way." I gave Asa a curious look.

Brannon spent the rest of dinner eating in silence while Asa and I spoke about her looking for a job. She even spoke of starting her own company.

Our tense dinner was quickly finished, followed by Asa clearing away the table while I fetched a brandy for Brannon. Grunting a thank you, he took the brandy but just placed it on the table while staring out the patio window.

I sensed a fight coming on, but I had to find out about the money, as bills were due. My money went to run the farm while Brannon's money paid for the household bills. I needed to know if I had to transfer money from the farm account into the household account. And frankly, I was getting irritated at his manner. "Brannon? Did you lose your checks or were they stolen?"

"No, I needed the money for something else."

"What was that?"

Brannon's skin reddened as he broke into a sweat. His face contorted until these words bubbled out of his mouth, "There's no point in putting this off." He placed a hand on mine. "I'm so sorry, Josey. Really I am, but I'm leaving."

"Leaving? You have a business trip?"

Brannon nervously tapped his brandy glass with his other hand.

"Brannon?" We stared at each other until Asa broke the silence.

"Mom. I think he's trying to tell you that he is leaving us." Her face had whitened into a pale mask as she peered out from the kitchen into the dining room.

I pulled my hand away. "Is that what you are trying to say? You're leaving me?"

Brannon nodded. "I wanted to tell you both together. I love you, but I hate my life here."

"You hate your life here?" I echoed, my voice becoming shrill. I couldn't breathe. It felt like someone had just pushed me off a cliff. "This has caught me totally off guard. I don't understand. How can you leave when the farm is saddled with debt and after what Asa's been through the last year? How can you leave us with all this going on?" I was bewildered.

"That's why he's leaving," sneered Asa. "It's too much for him. Daddy doesn't like complexity, do you? You like things simple without blemish. Right, daddy?"

"Now Asa, don't start," Brannon begged.

"It's true. I've embarrassed the family, you, even though I was innocent, but that didn't matter. It was a huge scandal. What must your friends have said to you at the country club?"

"That's not true," denied Brannon. "This has got nothing to do with you. It really has nothing to do with your mother. I just want to start fresh. I've been very unhappy for the past several years."

Asa and I glanced at each other.

"Is there someone else?" I asked, fearful of the answer.

"Of course not," Brannon said, standing up. "I'd better go. Everyone is upset. I will talk to you, Josey, when this calms down."

"Calms down? You've got to be kidding. Is there anything I can say or do that will make you talk this out?" I pleaded, reaching for him.

Brannon shrugged away my hand. "I'll call in a few days and let you know where I'm staying."

I literally wrung my hands not knowing what to do. Should I let him walk out the door? Should I beg him not to leave? Was he having a mental breakdown? What was the right thing to do? My hand dipped towards my chest as I listened to my ragged heartbeat.

I heard him go into our bedroom, get something and then leave by the bedroom patio door. "Oh my God," I whimpered, shutting my eyes.

Asa stormed into my bedroom. "MOM!" she cried. "You'd better see this."

I rushed into the bedroom and looked where Asa was pointing. I fell against the closet door in disbelief. Brannon had rummaged through my things and taken all my expensive jewelry, a coin collection that I was saving for Asa and several couturier vintage dresses. My things were strewn all over the floor.

"Why in the world did he take those things? What's he up to?"

"Mom, give me your account numbers. I want to get on the computer and check on all your accounts."

I numbly pulled a file from my desk drawer in my office, which gave her the code words. Within a half an hour, Asa came back with printed pages of all our savings funds. Brannon had taken money from each one of the accounts. There was almost nothing left. The only thing intact was my retirement fund, which he could not touch.

I threw the sheets on the floor in dismay. "He's not coming back, is he?"

Asa shook her head. "It seems like he has been planning this for a long time."

"But why? Where is all the money and why would he take my personal things?"

Asa led me to a chair and knelt down before me. "I don't know, Mom. But I'll find out tomorrow. Right now, we need to have the locks on the house changed."

"What? I don't know about that. Locking your father out of his own house?" What Brannon had done still hadn't registered.

"We need to move quickly and save what we can of your assets. I'm going to call a locksmith right now. I'll pay for it. Don't worry."

I heard Asa in the next room making several calls. Then she brought me a stiff bourbon. I drank it and then another. I wanted to get stinking drunk.

And I did.

Prologue
Again . . . just in case you forgot.

The dark-clad figure pulled out the wires to the security box. Deftly, the intruder cut the correct wire to silence the alarm. Then going around to the southwest part of the huge mansion built in 1832, the thief skillfully unlocked the side porch door and stepped into the library.

Hearing a dog growling in the hallway, the thief threw a piece of meat towards the hall and stood patiently until the dog ate the meat and a moment later groggily stumbled, falling asleep. It would sleep for several hours from the drug administered to the meat but would wake up unharmed.

The thief looked for a wall safe behind paintings and even tapped on the walnut paneling. Finding nothing, the dark figure concentrated on the desk, taking pictures of any checks, bank statements, investments that could be found. Then the thief copied the computer files onto a flash drive.

Several drawers were locked but it took the thief only seconds to break them open. Finding a handgun, the thief put it into a black bag, also several award silver trophies from a bookshelf.

Silently investigating the house, the thief went towards the front parlor. There the thief moved to the Duveneck painting hanging over the mantel. With quiet efficiency, the thief broke the frame and cut the painting from its stretcher. Rolled, the painting was placed in a tube the thief had brought.

Both the painting and the bag with the silver were lowered out a window.

Now unencumbered, the thief studied the massive staircase. Making a calculated decision, the thief leaped up the stairs, taking three steps at a time. Hiding in the shadows of the hallway, the thief saw that most of the upstairs doors were open.

Seeing what looked like a nightlight dimly peeping into the hallway, the thief surmised that it came from a child's room and headed for it.

The thief was right.

A boy, wearing Spider-Man pajamas, lay asleep in a bed designed to look like a racecar. The thief studied the child's features. Suddenly the thief's hand shot out, but only to pull the blanket over the little boy.

The sleek, black figure pulled away and went to look for the mother's room. Going next door, the thief discovered the mother of the boy asleep in her king size bed. She was wearing shorts and a sports bra. Like the boy, she had thrown off her blanket and lay sprawled across the bed, lightly snoring. A purse hung off a chair.

The thief claimed it and then went directly to a jewelry box sitting on the vanity, and took it downstairs. Pouring the contents of both the purse and the box onto the couch, the thief picked up several pieces of jewelry and a wallet, then fled out the side door. The thief was careful to lock it again.

Picking up the bag and tube, the thief absconded into the woods and to a country road where a black sedan was waiting. Flinging the goods in the trunk, the thief turned off the night goggles, throwing them on top of the sack. Starting with gloves, the thief took off the dark jumpsuit, revealing a casual fall outfit. The dark clothing was stuffed into a garbage bag and securely tied. The thief let long dark hair escape from a confining cap and got in the car, quietly shutting the door.

The driver looked at his boss. "Twenty-five minutes. What took you so long?"

"The painting was more trouble than I anticipated," lied Asa. "Let's move on down the road."

The car sped down Old Frankfort Pike with its lights off until it cut over the road to Midway.

Asa leaned back in the seat, smiling to herself. Ellen was going to be distracted as she was going to spend a great deal of time cleaning up the identity theft which was going to start occurring tonight. As for the jewelry and silver, Asa would stash it in her New York apartment's safe until she could have something made from the stolen loot. The credit cards would be given to her driver.

Forty-five minutes later, Asa boarded a Piper from a private airstrip in Scott County and flew to New York.

The employee made several outlandish purchases from Ellen's laptop with her credit cards and later dropped the cards on the floor of a disreputable drinking establishment in Covington.

Josiah Reynolds slept fitfully in her bed, never knowing that her daughter had been in Kentucky.

1

Doreen Doris Mayfield DeWitt tapped her tapered glossy ruby nails on the gleaming end table while watching the woman pace before her. Although she felt like swiping the woman with her claws, she remained passive, watching as her guest spewed forth countless words trying to explain her situation.

"You see, Doreen, I simply can't go on like this. I mean . . . well, I didn't mean to fall in love with Addison. It just happened. So I'm going to have to renege on our little agreement. It simply wouldn't be right."

"You mean the agreement where I paid you to seduce Addison and provide me evidence of adultery so I wouldn't have to give him part of my fortune according to my prenuptial with him?"

Lacey Bridges batted her large blue eyes. "Well, I never asked you why you wanted me to seduce Addison.

Is that why? You want to divorce Addison? Well, that's wonderful because I want to marry Addison. See – it works out for everyone."

"Except for evidence of adultery or abuse, I would have to pay Addison a substantial sum of my money – my family's money – if I initiate the divorce."

"You could always say that he hit you."

"Don't be ridiculous," snapped Doreen. "No one would believe that."

"Well, I don't know what to say. This is a pickle for you."

"Let's start with the money I've already paid you and the video you were supposed to make for me."

Lacey laughed. "Well, the money is gone . . . for clothes, you know. And the tapes – well, I had to destroy those, you see."

Doreen sighed. "Do you always have to start a sentence with 'well'?"

"What?"

"Never mind."

Lacey simpered. "It wouldn't do to insult me, Doreen. I haven't told Addison the truth yet, but I will . . . if you keep pushing me."

"Afraid that he might recoil from such a gold digger as you?"

"He would forgive me but it would slow up the divorce, that's for sure." Lacey searched in her purse for lipstick. "Well, the way I look at it, we can all get what we want. You get rid of Addison and I get him with a little bit of money. Oh, come off it. I'm sure you can spare some cash for Addison. Surely you want him to go out in style?" Lacey opened her compact and smeared on frosted pink lipstick. Dropping the compact and lipstick back into her purse, she stood satisfied with both her appearance and negotiation. "I'm sure we can work this out to our mutual satisfaction. All of this depends on just how badly you want to divorce Addison, doesn't it?"

Lacey placed a card on Doreen's antique end table. "Here's where you can reach me. I'm sure you'll see that I am right after thinking about it. Don't rise, please. I'll see myself out." She air kissed Doreen and then pranced out of the room.

Upon hearing the front door slam shut, Doreen stared into the fireplace, losing herself to the dancing flames . . . thinking, thinking, thinking.

She'd be damned before she gave one red cent to that worthless English hustler she'd married. Absent-mindedly she fingered the heavy gold ring on her right hand until she finally felt its weight pull on her. Lifting her hand up to her face, she opened the ring's secret compartment and smiled. Good thing she had always liked history or she never would have purchased a ring supposedly owned by Lucrezia Borgia.

Doreen laughed. "Now what would Lucrezia have done in my circumstance?"

It was very late when Doreen finally went to bed but not before she had concocted a plan. She would get rid of Addison and his obnoxious little bitch too. And no one would know that it was she who had pulled the strings of a perfect murder about to take place in the calm green rolling hills of the Bluegrass.

Kentucky is not called the dark and bloody ground for nothing.

2

History tells us that in 1775 Richard Henderson gave the Cherokees $10,000 in goods for a landmass below the Ohio River and between the Cumberland and Kentucky rivers. That was Henderson's first of many mistakes in creating a new nation, for the Cherokees did not lay claim to the land below the Ohio River – the Shawnees did. Not withstanding though, Henderson hired Daniel Boone to blaze the Wilderness Trail through the Cumberland Gap to claim his new country of Transylvania.

The Cherokee war chief Dragging Canoe is said to have warned Daniel Boone, "We have given you a fine land Brother, but you will find it under a cloud and a dark and bloody ground."

No truer words had ever been spoken. The fertile earth of Kentucky is saturated with the blood of Indian tribe fighting Indian tribe, pioneers slaying Indians, slaves murdering masters, the brother in Blue warring against the brother in Gray, and feuds over timber, tobacco, coal, bourbon and now drugs. There has always been violence bubbling up from the rich dirt of these luscious green covered hills.

The fact that several men have attempted to kill me attests to this. It is miraculous that I am still alive to tell the tale. Maybe the spirits of the land watch over because they favor me or perhaps my trials amuse them. Who knows?

But I'm alive. I intend to stay that way.

My name is Josiah Reynolds. I am a retired art professor who was named after a biblical king who was known for his righteousness. Like King Josiah, I believe in right and wrong. It takes a wise person to know the difference. Sometimes right and wrong look the same in the daylight, but opposite in the reflection of moonbeams.

I should know. I have bent the law to suit my own purposes.

Sometimes to right a wrong.

Sometimes to protect myself.

Sometimes to help a friend.

And at times, these are heavy burdens that can turn around and bite you in the ass.

The sun is going down over the gray limestone palisades. The pool lights have come on. The birds are flying to roost in the nearby walnut, oak and paw paw trees.

I'm sitting on the patio with a frosted silver glass filled with bourbon, sugar and crushed ice accompanied by a sprig of mint I pulled from the herb garden for a drink that is called a Mint Julep.

I'm ready to tell Addison DeWitt's story. It is a story about greed. Men have been killed for lesser reasons in this land, but all of them died bloodied like Addison.

Like so many other men, Kentucky snared Addison and then killed him . . . without remorse, without pity. She just grabbed him in her ancient claws like an osprey skimming fish in the Kentucky River.

But somehow evil is balanced in Caintuck.

Like I always said – there is justice and then there is Kentucky justice.

3

First of all, I have to tell you about myself. I am a person that is limited. That is – I'm crippled. Let's cut the crap with the silly euphemisms. I'm not "physically challenged." I'm not "handicapped." I'm not "disabled." I am crippled for life and bitter about it. Very bitter.

I was pulled off a cliff by a rogue cop who was trying to kill me. He almost succeeded. Crashing into trees on the way down cushioned my fall, but the result was that my body shattered into a thousand pieces. It is a miracle that I'm alive at all.

All my teeth had to be pulled and implants put in. I wear a hearing aid. Scars are still visible near my hairline. An ugly scar runs up my left leg and I limp. I have to use a cane. Sometimes if I'm tired, I still use my wheelchair.

I have headaches and my short-term memory sometimes cuts out. I can't always find the word I wish to use. It is frustrating to communicate. My hands tremble when I'm tired. I also have asthma, which makes things harder. And the worst – pain is the enemy I fight every day. If I didn't have the pain, everything else would be almost bearable.

Almost finished with year one of recovery, I still have another year to go.

To make things worse, the son of a bitch who did this to me is stronger than ever, in perfect health and is strutting around Lexington like a swaggering cock. He's out on bail. How in the hell did that happen?

Anyway, Jake had come back. He had spent the last several weeks getting me back on an exercise schedule and monitoring my medication. We had reestablished our professional connection, but the personal one was much tougher.

After our passionate reunion in the hospital, Jake hadn't touched me. I didn't mention it but I was disappointed. Nor did I question him about his wife. I figured that when he was ready, he would tell me. But as the days passed, I began to wonder whether I should ask him.

I took a long look in the mirror and decided to be happy that I had someone attending to me who cared. I was a mess physically and no prize to look at. My face was passable and even pretty when I put on makeup. I had lost a lot of weight but there was still no way I wanted Jake to see me naked.

I knew that he had in the past when tending to my needs. Maybe that is why he put on the brakes. I was too afraid to ask. Let sleeping dogs lie.

I was thinking about all this when the phone rang.

Jake answered. There was a brief discussion and then he hung up. He poked his head into my bedroom. "Detective Goetz wants to speak with you. He's coming down the driveway."

"I wonder if this is about O'nan," I ruminated.

Jake shrugged. "I'll go make some coffee."

I followed Jake into the great room and sat looking out at the patio with the black infinity pool. To the far left of the pool were bird feeders. Several downy woodpeckers were eating the suet hung from tree limbs. Their black, white and red feathers stood out against the fall foliage. It was the last gasp of warm weather before the fall gave way to the colder days. The trees were beginning their annual blaze of orange and yellow. It was going to be a pretty fall.

Shortly the doorbell rang and Jake let Goetz inside. If Goetz was surprised to see Jake again, he didn't show it.

Goetz lumbered to where I sat and pulled a chair next to me. He looked irritated as he mopped his shiny forehead. "Man, it's hot out there today," he said, more to himself than to me.

"The last gasp of summer," I concurred.

Jake brought out a tray with coffee, glasses with ice, canned soft drinks and a plate of cookies. He gave me a questioning look before leaving the room.

Detective Goetz poured a soft drink onto the ice and took a great swig. "Ahhh, that feels better," he commented before taking out his notebook and a nubby pencil from his coat pocket.

"Uh oh, I see the mighty notebook. I take it that you are not visiting me socially," I rasped.

"No ma'am. Here on official business."

"Then I can't answer any of your questions. You know that I don't talk to the police anymore without a lawyer present."

"Them," grimaced Goetz, waving his hand contemptuously. "Aren't you even curious about why I'm here?"

"O'nan?"

Goetz shook his head.

"Really?" Indeed, I was curious. "Okay, I'll bite."

"Someone broke into Ellen Boudreaux's house a couple days ago and stole credit cards, silver, jewelry. A lot of expensive stuff."

I couldn't help but grin. "Maybe there is a god."

"The curious thing about the robbery is that is was done by a professional and while everyone was in the house asleep. That kind of thing takes a lot of guts to do. Also only certain items were taken, like a Duveneck painting, not worth a fortune, but still expensive . . . and then only certain pieces of jewelry. Lots of good stuff left."

I merely nodded.

"Now, Miss Ellen tells me that the painting and stolen jewelry were gifts from Brannon Reynolds."

"So you think that I crept into Ellen's house with this bum leg and stole her goodies like a professional cat burglar."

"I didn't think you did it," replied Goetz. The accusation hung in the air.

"I think we have come to the point where we have to end our discussion, Detective."

"When was the last time you saw Asa?"

"She's not your guy. She hasn't been home in almost a month. You know that, and since when does a homicide detective care about a burglary?" I was really mad now. "I help you break Arthur Green's murder case and get my leg all busted up doing it, not to mention his murderer who tried to stove in my head with a shovel, and this is the thanks I get."

"I'm being nice here. You would rather someone else?"

"I'm sick of looking at your ugly mug."

"I'm telling you that Asa pulled off that job and Ellen Boudreaux is after her hide."

"Anytime someone spits on the sidewalk, Ellen is screaming that I or Asa did it. You know she blames me for Brannon's death."

"Josiah, her little boy told me that he woke up and saw someone who looked like Batman tucking him in. He said it was a woman who told him to go back to sleep."

My heart froze with fear. "A nightmare by a little child. No court is going to accept that."

"I'm just here to warn Asa that the big guns are coming."

"Jake!"

Jake strode into the great room and loomed over Goetz. "I'll show you the way out, Detective."

"Will you talk to her?" asked Goetz.

"I think she understands. She just gets mad when Miss Boudreaux is involved." They moved to the front double-steel door where they shook hands. Jake watched the monitors until Goetz left the property.

When Jake came back, I was eating cookies and throwing down a soft drink, which he snatched out of my hand.

I lunged for the glass but missed. "I need a sugar fix," I grumbled.

"You need to talk to Asa," he retorted. "You think she did it?"

"You know she did. Who else can get in and out undetected, knew which painting and jewelry were gifts from Brannon and dresses like a goth undertaker."

"Why?"

"Who knows?" I answered, throwing up my hands. "Probably because it amused her."

"Or maybe she knows that Ellen is ready to sue you and wanted to throw some obstacles in her path to slow down the process."

"What do you mean?"

"Goetz said that credit cards were stolen. I guarantee that Ellen will spend some time getting that mess straightened out first before she launches her lawsuit. Identity theft sometimes takes years to clear up. And if I know my boss, she took all the financial information she could."

"She's trying to find Ellen's Achilles heel."

Jake nodded in agreement. "Obviously she takes Ellen very seriously. Ellen is making noises that she is going to take the Butterfly away from the both of you. Asa is not going to let that happen. She can play very dirty if she has to. I think Ellen Boudreaux has made a dangerous enemy."

"What should I do?"

"We need to make contact with Asa and let her know what is going on, but I wouldn't use our cell phones or your land line." He though for a moment. "Let's go see Franklin."

Franklin, of course. Why hadn't I thought of that?

*

Franklin opened the back door and groaned. "What do you two alley cats want?"

Jake pushed my wheelchair inside. Crutches were too hard for me, so I used the wheelchair when venturing out.

Franklin gave the surroundings a quick glance before shutting the door. Thankfully he lived on the ground floor of a three-story apartment building on Second Street. The building had been a dorm for Transylvania University before it was converted.

Even though Franklin dressed like a precocious child, his apartment was tastefully decorated. The walls were painted a very pale yellow, which cheerfully went well with furniture covered in English chintz. On the repainted end tables, which had been rescued from Goodwill, were fresh flower arrangements and a picture of Matt, my best friend, in a sterling frame. There were very few knickknacks but expensive coffee table books were stacked here and there. In the hallway was a large system of shelves, which held book after book. Some of them were encased in glass, so I guessed that they were first editions. On the walls hung still lifes purchased from local artists.

So Franklin was a book and flower freak. I should have guessed.

Jake leaned over and murmured, "It looks like Laura Ashley threw up in here."

"I heard that, heathen," shot back Franklin. "Josiah, that wheelchair better not mark up my floors. I just had them done."

"I need to use your land line," I requested.

"Don't you have phone?"

"Not one that I can use."

"Is this something clandestine?"

I leaned forward. "Perhaps dangerous."

Franklin clapped his hands together. "I'm in."

"Won't that irritate Matt?" asked Jake.

"Haven't seen Matt in days, almost a week. For awhile after his little indiscretion with . . ."

I shook my head emphatically behind Jake.

"Someone besides moi, he was good as gold afterwards. Then he started getting distant again. I don't know if we are coming or going sometimes." Franklin flung himself dramatically on his couch. "Is he seeing someone? Tell me. I can face it."

"I haven't seen him either. I really don't think so, Franklin. I think he is just bogged down with work at the office."

"Swear?"

"Pinky swear," I replied. "Now where is the phone?"

Franklin handed me a touch-tone replica of the '60s pink Princess phone.

I gave him a look.

He shrugged. "I just had to have it."

"It's a little over the top. Talk about flaming. Why don't you just pin a sign to your back that says 'GAY'?"

"Ya wanna use it or not? Quitchyer griping."

I began dialing while signaling to Jake.

"Franklin, show me the rest of your place?"

Franklin's face broke into a brilliant smile. "I'd love to. Would you like to see my bedroom?"

"Let's start with the kitchen," grimaced Jake.

While they gabbed about cooking, I dialed Asa's secret number. When it was answered, all I said was "Rosebud."

4

I found Jake and Franklin in the bedroom. It was one of the most opulent rooms I had ever seen. There was a lead glass door leading out to a moss-covered brick patio with a jungle of huge potted cast iron planters accenting an old black wrought iron outdoor dining table giving the room a New Orleans kind of feel – old, extravagant, moist and kind of seedy. It was great.

The walls again were a very pale yellow, which played well against the antique four-poster bed's turquoise silk coverlet and very expensive cotton sheets. On the walls were abstract city landscape paintings of New Orleans from the '50s. The dresser held pictures of Franklin at various ages in silver frames – a little shrine to self-love.

All of Franklin's toiletries were placed on a gilded mirror along with antique silver and leather brushes. Alongside one wall were tall ivory beeswax candles sitting on stressed painted wooden candlesticks of various heights. The other wall was covered in antique mirrors.

"Franklin, you're a hedonist," I said, fingering the material of an overstuffed chair in the corner. I really wanted to check out his closets. "Who knew you had taste?"

"I think by my clothes you could tell that," he responded.

"Oh, yeah. Of course," I replied, rolling my eyes.

"Are you done?" asked Jake, not really interested in interior decorating.

"Yep," I replied.

"I'm hungry. Let's all get something to eat. My treat," said Jake.

"Sound great. We can just walk. There is a new restaurant on Jefferson Street at the corner."

"You guys go on. I'm going to drive the car there so Miss Daisy can go home right afterwards," suggested Jake.

"Okay," agreed Franklin as he opened the back French doors to let us out. Both he and Jake lifted my wheelchair on to the flat driveway. Franklin chatted happily as he pushed me along to the restaurant. I asked Franklin to go inside first to make sure there was room enough for the wheelchair to negotiate. Sometimes seating was so tight, a wheelchair couldn't make it to a table.

"Don't go anywhere," Franklin teased as he pushed the door open.

While waiting for him, I perused the street. There was another restaurant a half a block away. Hearing a familiar voice, my head swung towards it.

I could hardly believe my eyes.

It was Matt leaving the restaurant with a woman.

My gawd – it was Meriah Caldwell, the famous mystery writer!

They were laughing as he opened a car door for her. I watched him enter the driver's side, start the car and drive past only to catch the red light at the corner where I sat. Meriah was chatting up a storm as Matt grinned like a fool. Glancing out the window, he saw me staring at him.

Matt's expression froze.

The light changed and the driver behind him beeped his horn. Matt hurriedly drove away.

"Whatcha looking at?" asked Jake, coming up behind me.

"A firestorm," I replied.

Franklin stepped out and related to Jake that there was a handicap ramp in the back. Franklin went back in as Jake wheeled me around. My mind swirled.

Of all the women available – why Meriah Caldwell? Beside the fact that she was beautiful, successful and rich – what did Matt see in her?

I was flabbergasted. I was astonished. I was horrified. I was jealous.

Yes, I was jealous. I loved Matt deeply but I was not in love with him. But he was so beautiful and accomplished, my stomach turned anytime I saw him look at some other woman. Did I mention that he strongly resembled the '50s matinee idol Victor Mature? They could have been twins.

Like Victor Mature, Matt was from Louisville but that is where the resemblance ended. Matt took himself very seriously while Victor Mature was self-deprecating. Mature always said that he acted with his forehead. He was known to say, "Actually I'm a golfer. That's my real occupation. Ask anybody, especially the critics."

I knew Matt loved me too. I hated the thought that I might have to share that love. So like I said, I wasn't in love with Matt.

Was I?

5

"What are we playing at?" I finally asked Jake, as he was trying to get me ready for the night. He had ordered a hospital bed, which was easier for me to get into with my newly bummed-up leg.

"What do you mean?"

"Don't play games with me. Only a few months ago, you asked me out for a date." Seeing Matt today had made me bold.

"Did I?"

"Listen, nothing pisses me off more than someone trying to play me. What's going on? Why did you lie about being married?"

Jake sat on the bed and let out a long sigh. He rubbed his fingers through his long black hair. He wouldn't look at me.

"Jake? Talk to me."

"Every time I try to get close to you, something happens. It's like I'm bad news. Like something is trying to stop us."

"That is complete nonsense. I fell off a cliff. Where were you then? Hadn't even met yet. See, that had nothing to do with you."

"Then that Tavis tried to kill you."

"Whom you saved me from. These things would have happened anyway. I can't explain it. I have been living a half-life for the past few years with Brannon leaving me in total chaos. I had forgotten how to love, how to forgive, how to move forward with my life. Then I fell off a real cliff and who was there to guide me back to the land of the living? An uptight, brooding Indian."

"Native American."

"What?"

"We're called Native Americans, not Indians," replied Jake, turning his dark eyes intensely on me.

"Quit splitting hairs." I touched his fingers with mine. "You've healed me more ways than just my body. You healed my spirit, gave me hope. I want to love someone . . . even if it ends someday."

Jake remained still.

"I know I'm not young, and in pretty bad shape, but my heart can be as giving as the young or the beautiful. Oh, Jake, for goodness sake, say something. Don't let me babble on like this if you're not interested."

"I thought I was divorced. I didn't lie to you," Jake confessed. "When Asa told me that the papers hadn't been filed, I was humiliated. I knew how you felt about cheaters. I went home and confronted my wife. She had never filed the papers. She was having second thoughts."

"Didn't you suspect something was wrong when you didn't get the final decree?"

Jake shook his head. "I signed the papers overseas and gave instructions that the final decree should be sent to my mother's address. I wanted nothing more to do with it or my wife. I didn't even have my own apartment after I left her. Asa sent me straight to the Middle East to work on an assignment and then pulled me back to the States when you got hurt. I hadn't talked to my wife in almost two years. I thought it was over. I deposit money in her account once a month for the children and that is it."

"What about your children?"

"I talk to them all the time but we never discuss their mother. They know it is a sore spot. I've been home only a few times, and stayed at my mother's where they came to visit. Their uncle brings them. Like I said, I haven't seen my ex in almost two years."

"What happened?"

"She was banging some guy from work."

I said nothing, patiently waited for Jake to continue.

"I know how it feels to get kicked in the gut by someone you trusted. At least she didn't steal money like your husband did."

"And now?"

"The papers are filed. I made sure of that. I'm waiting for the final decree."

"Is that why you haven't brought up us?"

42

"I knew from kissing you in the hospital that you were pretty fragile again. I didn't want to start something we both can't finish." He gave a goofy grin. "I don't want to hold back and I don't want you to either."

"I'm in no shape?" I thought back to when I was with Matt. I had pretty much kept up with him in the bedroom, but I didn't dare disagree with Jake.

"Aw hell, you're months away. Why start something that is going to drive us crazy?" He gently touched my cheek. "You know?"

"I want to get this right. You're saying that we're an item but I need to get better before we start . . . convorting?" I looked at him curiously.

"Yeah. Something like that. But I will be here every step of the way for your recovery. You didn't break your leg – just a stress fracture. Let's get that healed first and work on getting your muscles in shape again." Jake held my hand. "I'm not leaving. I'll be here for you. You can lean on me." He kissed the palm of my hand and held it against his cheek. "I'm willing to take a chance on this. Are you?"

The one thing about getting older is that you realize that you take happiness where you find it. "Let's follow the sparks and see if a fire grows," I replied.

Jake kissed the inside of my wrist. He murmured, "So you want to see if a fire grows?"

I could feel my skin blushing from my back to my face. I was suddenly very warm.

He lingered on the inside of my elbow, showering it with baby kisses.

The doorbell rang. Jumping Jehosaphat!

Sighing, Jake rose and went to the front door.

I knew how he felt. It seemed like we never got a private moment. Every time we connected, something interrupted.

A few minutes later, Jake lounged against the doorframe. "Matt's here and is in a tizzy. He wants to see you now."

I groaned inwardly. I was hoping that a confrontation could be put off several days, maybe a week. There was no getting around this. "Help me get in bed first. Then let Matt come back."

Jake worked with me until I was finally comfortable. He shooed away Baby, my 225-pound mastiff, when he tried to climb in bed with me. Giving Jake a snotty look, Baby settled down in his own comfy bed, but not before turning three times.

Matt strode in. His black hair was accented by glistening mist as it had started to drizzle outside. His tie was off and several buttons of his shirt were unbuttoned. He looked dark. He looked sexually dangerous.

I couldn't help it. He simply took my breath away. I was ashamed of my feelings for him. It must be the same way with men. They love their wives dearly, but if given a chance, most couldn't pass up an hour with a Playboy girl. It must be in our genes to possess beauty, whatever form it comes in.

"Did you have dinner with Franklin?"

"Hello to you too."

"Did you?"

"Sure did."

"Did you tell him that you saw me?"

"With that skank? Nope."

Matt breathed with relief. "I've got to handle this carefully or it is going to blow up in my face."

My heart sank. "Was this more than just a dinner with a client?"

Matt looked at Jake leaning against the doorframe. "Do you mind, Jake? How about some privacy here."

"Leave this tender scene? No way."

Matt looked at me for backup but I shook my head. "He stays. What's going on, Matt?"

"I'm going to marry Meriah."

I cried out, "You can't be serious! Oh Matt, what have you done? Are you out of your mind?"

"I asked her tonight. She said yes."

I was dumbfounded. "Does she know about Franklin?"

"She said she didn't care."

"She's lying. Any woman would care that her fiancé had a male lover. Deeply care." Thousands of questions filled my mind. "How long have you been seeing her?"

"About three months. It just happened. We have common goals, similar interests. She's beautiful and . . ."

"Yadda. Yadda. Yadda. She's rich and can help you succeed. That's the bottom line."

"It's not. I'm in love with her."

"Oh please. You're talking to me, Matt. Me! Of all the women to marry, you pick that phony. Yes, a two-bit phony. She doesn't love you. Meriah likes your looks, baby. You're a prize trophy to show off to her Hollywood friends, and the fact that you're bi makes you all the more tantalizing. You're nothing more than a trophy to her."

"I was hoping that you would support me in this."

I laughed bitterly. "This is such a unexpected blow, I don't know what I'm going to do. What about Franklin?"

Matt shifted uneasily on the chair. "I'll take care of him."

"Oh, poor Franklin."

"Are you still going to be my friend? Are you going to stand by me?"

"Of course I am, you ass. But I'm not going to like it one bit. Not one bit."

Matt looked relieved. "Good. Then I expect you to come to our engagement party next Saturday at Lady Elsmere's house. Be there by eight-thirty. I'll send the Bentley."

"June knows about this?"

Matt nodded.

"I'll be there but I won't be pleasant."

"Just be there, Rennie," Matt said, calling me by his pet name for me.

"Matt. Please think this over. I'm begging you."

"It's done. I'm not turning back." He placed his hand on my shoulder. "Please, Josiah. Stand by me."

I acquiesced. I mean – what could I do? He had been my best friend since Brannon had left. Matt had stood by me through thick and thin. I had to be his friend in this even though it made me sick. What was I going to say to Franklin?

Like Scarlett O'Hara, I would think about that tomorrow.

6

It was Saturday night. The front lawn was covered in Mercedeses, Lexuses and an occasional beat-up farm truck. Jake took the car into the back where he could gather me into the wheelchair without a lot of gawkers. Once he had my green chiffon print dress folded to neatly cover my pink satin bedroom slippers, I straightened his tuxedo tie and together we boldly entered Lady Elsmere's house through the back sunroom, down the long marble hallway and into the grand foyer.

Spying us, Charles, Lady Elsmere's butler and right hand, hurried over with glasses of champagne and small plates of canapés so that it looked like we had been there for some time. We were terribly late and had gotten there just in time to hear Lady Elsmere give a toast to the engaged couple who were standing hand in hand on the stairwell.

Everyone drank but me.

I had to admit Meriah looked stunning in a white and gold lamé dress with a diamond hairpin borrowed from Lady Elsmere, aka June Webster from Monkey's Eyebrow, Kentucky.

Meriah's face was glowing and her tawny skin gleamed in the soft light provided by beeswax candles. For a moment I almost believed that she truly loved Matt, but deep down I knew better.

Matt surveyed the room until he saw me. His brooding face brightened.

I lifted my glass to him.

He gave me a slight nod of acknowledgement, which Meriah caught. Her head swiveled so fast I thought she'd get whiplash. I bit my lip so as not to giggle.

Everyone gathered to congratulate them and slap Matt on the back. Meriah was soon swept away by the "girls" who wanted to know all the "details" while Matt went to drink with the "boys" in the library.

Lady Elsmere walked over to me. "You're late."

I swiveled my wheelchair around. "You're right."

She flicked her hand at Jake. "You there. Go drinking with the rest of your kind. I want to talk to Josiah."

Jake gave me a quick kiss on the cheek and strode down the hall to join the rest of the men.

"I wish you'd quit talking to Jake as though he's a servant to do your bidding."

"So the Choctaw is back."

"June, don't piss me off. I'll ram your spindly legs with my wheelchair."

"I'm just showing you how you treat Meriah."

"I am very polite to her."

"Polite, cold and forbidding. You're not nice."

"You approve of this marriage? Oh, I forgot. You married a gay man, which is how you got your title."

"Don't be rude, Josiah. It may not have been the marriage that dreams are made of, but I loved my Bertie and he loved me. We made it work."

"She doesn't love Matt."

"How do you know? Are you such a magician that you can see into Meriah's heart? There are many kinds of love. Many kinds." She pointed a diamond-laden claw at me. "If you want to keep Matt in your life, make peace with her or you will force him to choose between the two of you."

I didn't have a chance to respond as we heard a door crash open. Matt ran down the hall shouting for Charles.

"What is it?" cried June, her diamond-laden hand jerking in concern to the thin red ribbons that made up her mouth.

"Call the doctor. Someone's having a fit," yelled Matt.

I wheeled past June and was soon in the huge library where a group of men were clustered. I wheeled across the expansive hardwood floor, around the couch and antique marble end table, through a knot of men.

Lying on the floor before a massive carved marble fireplace was Addison DeWitt with Jake hovering over him. Jake had taken his coat off and was protecting Addison's head while other men were holding Addison's twitching limbs. It was frightful to watch as Addison pitched, trembled and thrashed. Several men gave Jake pillows, which he put around Addison's head to cushion it. Another man took off Addison's shoes and loosened his belt and tie.

Other guests were on their cell phones calling 911. Charles and Matt ran in with some blankets and covered the fact that Addison had soiled himself.

By now, the women were pushing through the doorway. Matt stopped them. Pulling Meriah aside, he asked her to take the ladies back into the parlor; they were simply getting in the way. Like a pro, Meriah herded the whispering and confused ladies back down the hallway – all that is, except Doreen DeWitt, who now stood with the little crowd of men, looking frightened. She kept whispering something over and over.

Suddenly a chill ran down my spine. Something was off . . . like when someone sits next to you at a party and something in your gut tells you to move. You may not be able to put the correct name to it, but you realize something evil is near you. I was sensitive to things not being right. I made it my business anymore.

What was out of kilter?

All of a sudden, the twitching stopped. Jake checked Addison's eyes and leaned over to hear if he was breathing. He instructed the man helping him to press on the chest when he gave the word. Then Jake bent over to give mouth-to-mouth. They kept at until the ambulance came, but Jake shook his head when he caught my eye.

Doreen let out a wail and tried to lay down with Addison's body as the ambulance crew tried to revive him to no avail. She eventually had to be given a sedative by the paramedics, and was taken upstairs as the police walked in the front door.

The cop who strode through the door was Officer Kelly. He gave me a quick look, but we acted as though we didn't know each other. He asked Charles what the problem was. They whispered for a long while in a little huddle.

I wondered who had called him. This wasn't a police matter, but a medical one. Wasn't it?

It wasn't long before Officer Kelly ordered the men into the parlor with the women and cordoned off the library.

Kelly told me to "get thee to the parlor." Of course, when his back was turned, I wheeled straight to the kitchen and got a plate of hot food. I was starving. Charles' wife was putting things away until Officer Kelly walked in and told her to join the guests as well. "You too, buddy," he said curtly to me.

I took several more mouthfuls as Kelly started pushing my chair out the door. "Kelly. Kelly," I said in a stage whisper. "Something's odd about that man's death."

"Why?" he asked out of the corner of his mouth.

"I just know it. The room felt creepy."

After he rolled me into the parlor with the others, Kelly called Goetz.

"I've got a dead body."

"Yeah?"

"It looks like a heart attack to me, but Josiah Reynolds is here. She thinks something is wrong. Says the room felt creepy. I've known her since I was fourteen. Mrs. Reynolds has good instincts."

There was silence for a few seconds before Goetz responded. "I'll be right there."

7

Meriah was sitting in a corner with Lady Elsmere, both of them looking contrite, with Matt hovering over them. I was stationed near a window watching the coroner take Addison DeWitt's body out to his van, but not before Goetz pulled up and spoke with him. The coroner shook his head. Looking up, Goetz saw me in the window and gave a curt nod. The forensic guys pulled up behind him. They put on booties and paper jumpsuits before heading in.

I heard footsteps pacing upstairs where Doreen had been taken. Obviously she was looking out the window too. Very alert for someone who had been sedated. I whispered to Jake, who discreetly left the drawing room by the back door and headed to the second floor by the servants' stairs.

A few minutes later, Jake popped up by my side. He indicated that Charles' wife was with Doreen, which explained the foot traffic. Oh well.

One by one the guests were taken into another room and then let go, but not before all the glasses in the parlor and library had been collected and bagged. Finally it was Meriah, Matt, June, Jake and I left in the room. We huddled together in a sad little group saying nothing until Matt spoke, "I'm sure everyone is exhausted. I know I am."

"It's been over three hours," complained Meriah. "What are the police doing?"

"This is just dreadful!" exclaimed June. "I liked Addison so much."

"What about Doreen?" I asked. "What are you going to do about her?"

Matt scratched his forehead. "I can take her home. I've already called her daughter. She'll be waiting at Doreen's house."

I looked at Meriah and June. "Would you both be more comfortable at my house until Charles can put everything back in order? It would be no bother."

June patted my arm. "Thank you, Josiah, but I want to be in my own bed. Maybe Meriah?"

"I think I will stay with June," answered Meriah, giving a conciliatory look to Matt.

"How are you holding up, Rennie?" asked Matt.

I grimaced. "Hanging in there, but my energy is draining fast."

"It hits her like a wall. She'll be fine one moment and then bam, just like that, done for the day. I wish the police would hurry this up," concurred Jake. "I'm getting tired myself."

"You know," ventured Meriah, "there's something about this that's not right."

"Why do you say that, darling?" asked Matt.

I was curious myself as to what her perceptions were.

"Doreen was at the end of our little procession down the hallway, like she was deliberately hanging back till the end. Then when we got to the library's doorway, she pushed through past me and entered the room."

"So?" said June.

"I stopped right in the doorway, didn't I, honey?" she asked Matt.

"I didn't notice," replied Matt.

"You did stop right in the doorway with several other women. I was already in the room when your group came," I confirmed.

A cop opened the door and ordered. "Sorry. No talking, folks."

"How much longer?" asked Jake.

"We're done when we're done," answered the cop.

"These women can't take much more," protested Matt angrily.

Goetz appeared at the doorway. "Let me apologize. I know it's getting late. We will be done very shortly." He motioned to Jake and me. "Can I talk to you both?"

I bade everyone good night and followed Goetz into the next room.

He sat in a green leather chair and studied his notes under the end table light.

Jake stood behind my wheelchair, refusing to sit.

"Okay," said Goetz, finally looking up. "Everybody I talked to thinks Addison DeWitt either had an epileptic fit or a heart attack. Not one person mentioned foul play."

I just shrugged. "What do you think?"

"A heart attack. However, to be sure, we will do an autopsy, and have the food and liquor checked."

"Be careful with those glasses. They're antique crystal," I reminded him.

"We won't hurt Lady Elsmere's precious cocktail glasses." Goetz scratched his nose. "We will be checking with everyone in a couple of days to see if anyone else has had any ill effects. Right now tell me what happened."

Jake and I gave a quick recap of our attendance at the party, which Goetz put down in his worn out notebook and then gave us the nod to leave.

As we were leaving, I glanced up the grand staircase.

Standing in the shadows of the balcony was Doreen, watching silently.

It gave me the heebie-jeebies. I couldn't wait to get home.

There to greet us was Baby, thumping his tail loudly against the wall as he wagged it. I gave him a big hug to which he returned my affection by burying his snout in my crotch. Thanks.

I watched Jake check all the monitors, punch in the security code and, after he wheeled me into my bedroom, check all the doors and windows. I could tell that he was spooked too. Nobody likes to see a man die.

After Jake put me to bed, I asked, "Jake, do you mind sleeping in my room tonight? I've got the jitters."

"No problem," grinned Jake. He quickly changed and came back into my room wearing gym shorts and a tee shirt.

He pushed my Hans Weger bed next to the hospital bed and climbed in after turning off the lights. Baby whined until Jake gave him the green light to climb in as well. Happily Baby stretched out full length against Jake and was contently snoring within a few minutes. Baby's entourage of cat buddies joined him. Some fell asleep on top of Baby's rib cage, one straddled his head and several curled between his massive paws.

They were born in my closet on my favorite cashmere sweater and I have not been able to get rid of them since. After an appropriate age, I rounded them up and took them to the barn, but that evening they showed up at the back bedroom door, meowing to be let in. To add to this pitiful scene, Baby paced back and forth from me to the door, whining, until I caved and let them in. It is now a ritual. I put them out in the morning and they come back at the gloaming time, meowing for Baby.

I understood the need for company, especially on a chilly night.

Moonlight twisted through the large glass door that led out to the patio. Jake reached up searching for my hand.

Finding his, I clasped tightly, falling into a fitful sleep.

8

The next afternoon my carcass was parked in June's boudoir watching her eat breakfast in bed. June's boudoir was not like other people's bedrooms.

When my late husband, Brannon, remodeled her antebellum house, June gave implicit instructions about how she wanted the master suite. As a young girl, the bedroom of Rebecca DeWinter in Alfred Hitchcock's *Rebecca* had struck her fancy, so she had Brannon build a replica of the room with large floor-to-ceiling windows that opened onto a private balcony complete with the sheer white curtains that blew like twisting ghosts in the wind. The walls were adorned with imported silk fabric mimicking silver and pink cherry blossoms with antique Persian rugs riding the hand-distressed white plank floor. The furniture was painted silver with mirror accents. A silver silk comforter accompanied pale pink satin sheets.

The room was complete with a sitting area with a large carved white marble fireplace, which accented a portrait of Lady Elsmere in younger days over the mantle. To the right of the sitting room was a hidden door, which led to two large walk-in closets, jewelry safe and a small pantry that held snacks, cold drinks, and of course, chilled wine and champagne.

Finally the bathroom, which was the size of my bedroom at the Butterfly. It was made from white Italian marble – that means everything. The wall and floor tiles, the full-immersion tub and the steps leading into it, the hand carved sinks and the Roman shower. In addition, there was a fireplace and several phones lying about. It also boasted a bidet, but my favorite was the toilet with the heated seat, which sprayed scented warm water onto June's wrinkled bum. There was not a single roll of toilet paper in this bathroom.

Towels, soaps and rugs carried out the pink and silver motif of the bedroom.

In addition to this suite was a maid's/nurse's room with a private bathroom. Sometimes Charles' daughter, Amelia, stayed there if June was having a bad night.

And I thought my bedroom suite was pretty swanky.

Brannon had to build an entirely new wing on the house to accompany this dream; then he had to build a wing on the other side of the house for symmetry's sake in order to keep the integrity of the 1841 mansion intact. That wing housed the new kitchen, pantries, storage room, office, servants' quarters, servants' break

room, laundry facilities and mudroom. It was the
workhorse section of the house.

Luckily for me, the house also had an elevator, which is
why I was now up in June's bedroom pinching
strawberries from her floral, English morning pattern
china.

June picked up her phone and called downstairs.
"Would you please bring Mrs. Reynolds a breakfast tray
and some strawberries for me. Thank you."

"It's tea time. I've already had breakfast."

"Bring Mrs. Reynolds some finger sandwiches and hot
tea please, but I still want my strawberries. Thank you,
Amelia."

June looked at her clock. "I couldn't get to sleep last
night. How dreadful having something like that happen
in one's own home."

I snatched another strawberry.

"I do wish you'd eat at home, dear, and leave my
breakfast alone. By the way, what's with the leg?"

I looked down at the Velcro splint boot. "Coming
along nicely. It was a stress fracture rather than a break."

"Those are still serious. Take it easy."

"That's why I'm in a wheelchair instead of using my
crutches. I'm a klutz with them."

"Hmmmm," replied Lady Elsmere, buttering her toast.
I poured coffee into her cup.

"I suppose you are here nosing around."

"Nothing else to do."

"Could it be that you are here to get the dope on
Meriah and Matt?"

I shrugged. Leaning forward, I stirred cream in her coffee. "Do you know anything about them, June?" I asked.

"Why don't you ask me?" said Meriah as she strode into the room. She leaned over and kissed June on the top of the head.

June chortled as I felt the heat rise on my face.

"Okay. Why marriage?" I asked.

"Because Matt asked me," replied Meriah, returning my gaze calmly.

"You've been married twice before and that never took. You must know about Matt's . . . proclivities. Why take the chance? Tell us, June, did Lord Elsmere's tastes change after he married you?" I asked.

"I'm not going to get into this catfight, but I will tell you one thing. This marriage is none of your business, Josiah. Matt didn't ask you to marry."

I opened my mouth to speak and then shut it. June was right. It was none of my business, even though I knew nothing good would come from it. "My apologies, ladies," I said. "I should have just kept my mouth closed."

"Well, that's a first, coming from you," spat Meriah.

"Play nice," admonished June. "Ahh, here is your tea tray, Josiah."

Never one to refuse free food, I brightened. A table with the tray was placed before me. It was loaded with little sandwiches and cakes plus a big pot of hot tea and my honey.

"You want something, Meriah?" I asked.

Abigail Keam

"I couldn't possibly. My figure. You go ahead as I can see that you are not concerned about yours," she stated.

Before I could reply, she swept out of the room. To make a point I crammed a cucumber sandwich in my mouth.

June laughed before begging for an éclair. With reluctance, I passed a small one to her. I'm very stingy with pastries.

We chitchatted about the party and June related some awful stories about Doreen DeWitt. Awfully good, that is.

Doreen was an heiress with only one daughter from her first marriage. She had married against her family's wishes by running off with the chauffeur – literally. It turned out that the man had a natural ability with money and turned her little inheritance into a great big fortune by pulling her funds out of IBM and AT&T and putting them into companies like Microsoft in the '80s, and then again pulling out before tech stocks took a hit. Most of her money was now sitting in long-term CDs with six percent or better interest. It is rumored that her big mansion, her expensive cars and her jewelry are all paid for – no debt.

Unfortunately, her wise husband didn't make it to see his daughter graduate from a big ivory tower school before he died of brain cancer.

After mourning for a suitable period of time, Doreen took up with a handsome TV star whom she met at a Kentucky Derby party. He had a bad gambling problem, which was kept hidden until he had access to Doreen's money. After he had paid off his bookies, loan sharks and past girlfriends who had given him money, Doreen's fortune had taken a big hit. Needless to say, after receiving a few bank statements, she got rid of him quick.

"Doreen changed after that," remarked June. "She became obsessed with money . . . or rather with keeping it. It has been years since I have seen Doreen pick up a lunch tab or give to a charity. I just don't call her anymore for fundraisers. She is so cheap she won't even give her old coats away to the needy. She goes to Florida for a few months every year and that's the most exciting thing she does. Doreen is a rather boring woman, I'm afraid to say. You know, poor is a state of mind but broke is only a situation. Doreen is a poor person no matter how much money she has."

"What about Addison? I though he was rather dashing. She had to have something to attract him."

"She brought that man back from Florida complete with a tan, English accent and exquisite manners. I don't know how that charming man stood her," complained June, ringing for her tray to be taken away.

I heard the elevator switch on.

"I'd best be going," I said, putting down my napkin. "Jake is cooling his heels in the kitchen."

"Thanks for checking on me."

"Always, darling."

"Josiah, remember my advice about Meriah."

"I will. I'll be good from now on."

June chortled, "That will be the day."

I wheeled into the hallway and greeted Amelia coming to collect the trays. We spoke for a few moments before moving on. Amelia also worked as a docent on the Butterfly tours. It was from Amelia or Charles that I got the goodies of what was really happening in the "big house." She had just given me some interesting dope on Doreen DeWitt and June's latest houseguest.

As I started to get into the elevator, Meriah stepped out of her bedroom and beckoned to me. Curious, I pushed myself down the expansive hallway and into her room.

Unlike June's girlie motif, Meriah's room was very masculine with dark green walls and heavy traditional furniture. Meriah seemed at ease in it. Obviously her taste was more conservative than Lady Elsmere's.

"Josiah, can we make peace?" asked Meriah. "This snapping at each other is not good."

"I don't know about that," I replied. "I feel pretty good insulting you."

"You don't think highly of me, do you?" pouted Meriah.

"I don't think of you often, but when I do, it's not favorable. Over the past year or so, you have latched onto an old lady who is lonely and you have played that card to the hilt. I understand that you have not paid for one darn thing since you have been in this house. The least you can do is take June out for lunch now and then to repay her kindness.

"Then you have tried to interfere in my life by writing about it for your pulp novels. Tacky. I also know from a few verbal slips here and there that you tried to move in on Jake. When that didn't work, you obviously moved on to Matt."

"I'm impressed. How do you know about Jake? Did he tell you?"

"You mentioned one of Jake's tattoos some months ago at the Morris Book Shop. You can only see that tattoo if he is . . . unclothed. My guess is that you came to the house when you knew I would be napping and caught him unaware in the pool or the outdoor shower. He told you to go to the Devil, didn't he, Meriah?"

"Touché," cooed Meriah. "You have a very good analytical mind. I do like the exotic, but I got turned down flat. It rather hurt my pride. But I didn't go after Matt. He came after me. It was during your party for Franklin when I choked on that woman's awful glass eye and Matt saved me. Later that night, he called me up for a date and things proceeded from there. Now that's the truth."

"Matt called you up?"

"Yes. He was handsome. He was single. He asked me out to dinner. I was bored so I went. We had a good time. He asked me out again. I went again. Matt pursued this. Not me."

I didn't reply. Actually I was rather stumped, but I shouldn't have been. Matt had been struggling for a long time.

"Do you love him?"

"You are right to think that I am a selfish woman. I am. But Matt is as ambitious as I am. We have the same goals. We will work well together as partners because as ambitious as Matt is, he's very old school. He will rub the rough edges off me."

"You're hoping that Matt will make a lady out of you?"

"No. I'm hoping that he will make me kind."

I gave Meriah a long hard look. She was a drowning woman clutching onto the only thing floating in the ocean. She was looking to Matt to save her from herself. I understood. I was doing the same with Jake. When the possibility of happiness comes your way, you grab onto it. It was human nature.

"Okay," I said.

"Okay what?"

"A truce. I won't interfere and I wish you both happiness. If this is what Matt wants, then I want it for him."

Meriah sighed. "Thank you. Your acceptance will make things easier for Matt."

"Where will you live?"

"We are going back to my house in California after we are married. Matt already has a job offer in a good law firm there. He'll fit right in."

"I see."

Nothing stayed the same forever. I had to accept it.

"Now that is resolved, I want to mention something that has been troubling me."

"Oh?"

"It's about Doreen DeWitt."

"Go ahead." My mind was still reeling from the fact that Matt was going to move across the country, but I would give Doreen a go.

"Was there anything that troubled you about Addison DeWitt's death?"

"I got a creepy feeling that night." I searched for the right words. "Something seemed icky about the entire situation."

"Icky? A former college professor like you uses the word icky?"

"I think icky describes accurately what I was feeling."

Meriah pushed back her honey-streaked hair. "I was feeling something icky too, but about Doreen. When we heard the commotion, I was first out the door as I was the closest. Doreen was way on the other side of the room. She would have been one of the last to enter the hallway." She paused for a moment and then went to stand in her own doorway. "Now I stopped right in the doorway, didn't I?"

"I guess so. I was really paying attention to Addison."

"Well, I did. You even said so the other night. Now I stood in the doorway with a couple of other women who were not Doreen DeWitt."

"Okay."

"Now out of nowhere, Doreen pushes through and runs over to Addison DeWitt."

"That I remember," I concurred.

"Here's what is icky. How did she know it was Addison on the floor? I am taller than she but I couldn't see who was on the floor because the couch was in the way as were men also blocking my view."

"That's right. I had to wheel around the couch and there were men standing between the couch and Addison on the floor. I couldn't tell who it was until I pushed through the group of men." I paused for a moment. "She must have heard Matt yell to Charles in the hallway that Addison was having a fit."

Meriah shook her lovely head. "No one heard exactly what Matt said. It was muffled. We just heard the commotion and Doreen certainly didn't react to anything until we get to the library door."

"Wait a minute," I said correcting myself. "Matt didn't mention Addison's name. He just said someone was having a fit, so Doreen couldn't possibly have known he was talking about Addison."

"Precisely," Meriah continued. "So Doreen pushes through, starts calling Addison's name before she could see who it was. It's the timing of her awareness of Addison that is off."

"Maybe she stood on her tiptoes. Maybe she stood on a chair to look into the room."

Meriah shook her head. "I tried standing on my tiptoes and I could not see. And there was no chair out of place in the hallway that I noticed." Meriah stepped into the room and began pacing. "And all that crying and moaning and carrying on when Addison died. I don't buy it. Most women would have been weeping for sure but they also would have been in shock . . . in disbelief."

"They would have wanted someone to comfort them, like a family member."

Meriah snapped her manicured nails. "Quite right. She didn't ask anyone to call her daughter. Matt just took that upon himself."

"And she didn't go to the hospital that night either."

"Well, she was sedated."

"Was she? I saw her in the upstairs hallway as I was leaving. She was wide-awake, watching from above. And I talked to Amelia just a moment ago. She told me that she found a white pill in the heat register this morning when she was tidying up."

"A sedative pill?"

"She confirms that the doctor gave her a pill, not a shot, and that Doreen must have hidden it in the closed heat register when no one was looking."

"Does she have the pill?"

I shook my head. "She has emptied the vacuum cleaner. It hadn't occurred to her that the police might be interested in this pill."

"Or perhaps that June gave the order to destroy any unusual contents in that room. She doesn't want the coroner to rule anything but accidental."

We both were quiet, preoccupied with our own thoughts, until Meriah spoke. "You have contacts in the police department. Why don't you give them a call?"

The thought of getting involved in another murder was overwhelming. I was still worn out like an old dishrag. "Sorry. I have other fish in the frying pan. You will have to go solo on this." I wheeled towards the door before turning. "Meriah, I do wish you and Matt well. I hope you find happiness."

Meriah's fine features softened. "Thank you, Josiah. I wish you well too."

I nodded and left, harboring no ill feeling against Meriah anymore. She may have been beautiful and rich but she was alone, wary of the future and doubtful of her ability to meet it head on. She needed backup, which was Matt.

I knew what it was to be alone. After Brannon left me, so did most of our friends. Only Matt and Lady Elsmere had stuck by me. She once left a fifty thousand dollar check on my Nakashima table to "tide me over." I never cashed it, but it's in my drawer of keepsakes.

Things went into a tailspin after Brannon left. He refused to give me money, instead wanting me to sell the Butterfly. With co-workers and students cruelly snickering about Brannon's affair at work and meetings, I retired from teaching, feeling humiliated. Then I found Richard Pidgeon dead in one of my hives . . . you know the rest.

Yes, I harbored no resentment against Meriah. How could I? She was afraid, just like me.

9

I was getting used to my Velcro splint so I was flying solo while Jake took much needed time off. Charles helped me into my golf cart and put the wheelchair in the back as I was leaving the big house.

"Charles, do you know what Addison was drinking the night he died?"

"Bourbon neat."

"Are you sure? Maybe he had something different in the library?"

"Addison DeWitt drank bourbon neat that night. He didn't even have champagne for the engagement toast as he refused the glass I offered. I make it my business to notice what people drink at these parties. It's my job."

"Where was Doreen during the toast?"

"Standing next to Mr. Addison and she was drinking champagne for the toast." Charles thought for a moment. "She was also drinking the same bourbon that night as her husband."

"It stands to reason that maybe he was holding her bourbon drink while she toasted the champagne to the engaged couple."

"Maybe. I didn't notice. You came in and I went to get drinks for you."

"Yes. I remember. Just one more thing. If Addison wanted his drink freshened, would you have given him another in a new glass or topped his off?"

"There weren't that many people there, so I didn't need a bartender. I just freshened people's drinks or they could do so themselves at the little bar in the drawing room. Glasses were not being switched out."

"Was port or brandy served in the library?"

"Mr. Addison didn't like either of those drinks. He was strictly a bourbon man."

We chatted for another moment about the party before I headed for June's training track. Charles told me that Shaneika and Mike Connor were there watching Comanche workout.

I headed over, dodging workers walking with horses along the way, until I spied Shaneika, Mike . . . and Velvet Maddox, the dowser. Beside Mike's towering figure, she looked like one of the "wee people" the Irish reminisce about.

Slowly edging the golf cart towards them, I stopped at the railing, remaining quiet as they watched Comanche sprint around the track. After the sweating horse passed us, Mike pushed on the stopwatch. I could tell that Shaneika and Velvet were not happy by what they saw on the watch.

"What do you think?" asked Mike of Miss Velvet.

"I don't know at this moment. He has all the makings of a champion but he just doesn't seemed interested."

"Do you think something is wrong with him?" asked Shaneika in her British clip.

"Not physically," replied Velvet, scratching her chin. Her skin's consistency reminded me of biscuit dough. "I've checked him out and he's sound as a bell. What does your vet say?"

"That he is just a dud."

"Did you tell Miss Velvet about Comanche's companion goat getting murdered in front of him?" I asked, interrupting their conversation.

"What was that?" asked Velvet, looking surprised. "He saw his friend being murdered?"

I quickly relayed how George Fanning snuck into my barn and tortured one of Comanche's companion goats, finally slitting her throat. Then Comanche was moved to another training facility where a man was murdered and hung from the rafters.

"Well, that's the place to start," replied Velvet. "This horse could be traumatized."

Mike snorted in disbelief, upon which Miss Velvet turned on him. "I'll thank you to keep a civil tongue in your head, Mike Connor. You don't understand everything there is to know under heaven and earth."

Looking chastised, Mike coughed up, "I didn't say a word."

"I heard you loud and clear. You have no idea the pain we cause animals without blinking an eye at the harm we do. Do you not think a person would be sick at heart if he had seen two murders? Horses are just like people in being very sensitive to their environment."

"What would be the plan of action?" asked Shaneika. "Everything I've got is tied up in that horse. I can't quit now."

Miss Velvet narrowed her eyes. "You may have to. If that horse doesn't have it in him to win, you would just be throwing good money at him. I will have to talk to him and see what is up."

Shaneika shot a curious look at Mike.

"Of course, you can beat him with a crop until he does what you want," said Velvet.

The jockey brought Comanche to where we were gathered. Comanche reached over to nuzzle Shaneika for peppermints, which she always kept in her pocket.

"I'm not going to beat an animal to make him perform. You just better come up with something," demanded Shaneika.

The jockey and Mike exchanged comments until the jockey started the horse towards the stable.

"I've got tomatoes to can so I'll be off," announced Miss Velvet. "I'll be back tomorrow morning. No training, you hear."

"Yes ma'am," replied Mike.

Shaneika started to object but thought better of it. She didn't seem to want to take Miss Velvet on. She waited until the tiny woman had hopped into her huge pickup truck and blazed down the gravel road.

"I swear that old bat is crazy," she said turning on Mike. "She is gonna 'talk' to Comanche?"

"Okay. Do things your way but that old woman understands things that ordinary people just don't. I've seen her work wonders with horses."

"Any horses that won a race?" Shaneika stumped off muttering, "Crazy old white woman. Crazy Irishman."

I started to laugh until I saw Mike's fallen face. Uh oh. Mike had the look of a puppy that had been denied a juicy bone. I bade my goodbye to Mike, who barely took notice of me as he watched Shaneika storm away. I hurried away in my golf cart, not wanting to witness Mike's humiliation. I sure hoped Velvet Maddox made good with the horse – or Mike would never make good with Shaneika.

10

Asa sat in the parked SUV and checked her makeup. It was perfect. Instead of the usual kohl rimming her eyes, there was minimal of mascara and just a hint of lipstick. Her face was scrubbed free of makeup into a fresh hue, allowing the freckles on her nose to show. A brown curly wig, giving her a soft feminine look, concealed her dark long hair.

Instead of the usual black that she wore, Asa had chosen carefully. She was wearing beige slacks, a white silk blouse and a cardigan sweater with horses on it. Her jewelry was demure – gold post earrings, an emerald-cut engagement ring and a gold bracelet. Her bag and shoes were expensive but not over the top. She looked like the perfect up and coming Junior League wife.

Her companion commented, "You look just like the girl next door."

Asa blew him a kiss.

They both got out of the SUV and, acting like a loving couple, entered a popular Lexington restaurant in the Lansdowne Center.

The hostess, having been generously tipped previously, placed the couple in the middle of the room, where everyone could see them.

Even Ellen Boudreaux, who was having her usual Thursday lunch with her girlfriends. Ellen caught sight of her as soon as Asa entered the room. "I can't believe she would show her face in this town after what she did to me," growled Ellen, staring in partial disbelief.

"Who?" asked a girlfriend.

"Asa Reynolds!"

The entire table rubbernecked to where Ellen was pointing.

"That doesn't look like Asa Reynolds. You must be mistaken," declared another girlfriend.

"I'm telling you that is Asa Reynolds over there," spit Ellen, her face contorting into a Feliniesque mask. "I should know what my stepdaughter looks like."

Several of the women glanced at each other, knowing that Ellen never actually married Brannon Reynolds.

One of her girlfriends placed a hand on Ellen's arm. "Now, you have no proof that she broke into your house," she warned. "Just ignore her. We'll finish our lunch and then leave."

Worried, another woman commented, "Don't look, Ellen. People are starting to stare." She waved her hand at their waiter, wanting to get the bill and get out.

Asa laughed at something the man said.

"You have no idea of what she has done to me. My finances are all screwed up because of that bitch. I have to pay everything in cash until this identity theft mess is over and I'm told it is going to take months to straighten out, never the mind the valuables she took. Jewelry that Brannon had given to me. A valuable painting."

The others murmured in sympathy. It's not that they didn't believe that Asa had been behind the robbery at Ellen's house, but being lawyers' wives, they also knew that knowing something was not proving it. And they simply didn't like Ellen enough to be caught in a public fight with Asa Reynolds . . . if that was really Asa.

They quickly paid for their half-eaten lunches and pulled Ellen with them as they began to leave. But Ellen was just as Ginny Wheelright had described at Franklin's party – cunning but not bright. She just couldn't resist the temptation of confronting Asa.

She pulled away from her friends' grip and strode over to Asa's table. "I can't believe you would show your face in Lexington," sputtered Ellen.

Asa looked up in surprise. "What?"

"You heard me. After what you did to me, you show up like nothing's happened. Everyone knows you did it."

The man posing as Asa's fiancé interrupted, "Excuse me, Miss, but you're upsetting my fiancée. We don't want any trouble."

"Your fiancée?" sneered Ellen. She grabbed at Asa's ring hand.

"Stop it!" cried out Asa, pulling away. "Go away. Please."

Calling for the manager, the fiancé threw down his napkin. But before the manager could rush to the table, Ellen had picked up Asa's water glass and thrown water in her face.

The entire restaurant, which was now watching, gasped.

The boyfriend threw himself between Ellen and Asa, making sure he did not touch Ellen. He turned and helped Asa wipe the water off her clothes. The manager grabbed Ellen by the arm and escorted her to her friends waiting in the parking lot.

The friends murmured a few goodbyes after checking that Ellen was okay, but then took off like bats out of hell on a hot night. They certainly didn't want to be standing with Ellen if Asa Reynolds came out. She was known to have a hair-trigger temper.

Seeing that she was alone, Ellen reluctantly got in her Mercedes and left. Without her friends to cover her back, she didn't want to encounter Asa either. Confused and angry, she drove out of the parking lot.

After waiting several minutes, Asa and her companion threw a couple of twenties on the table and left the restaurant. Asa was plainly in tears – that is, until she got in the car. With the plan going as intended, she headed to the police station to file an assault complaint against Ellen. Now Asa just had to wait for the rest of her strategy to take place.

About a half hour later, when they had finished their lunches, five young drama students sitting in five different areas of the dining room paid for their meals and left. Each thinking that they had been contacted by a flash message earlier that day to tape a theater performance at a local restaurant, they went directly to their computers to download Ellen's attack on Asa to YouTube.   Five different perspectives. Five different angles. Then they buzzed it to their friends, who enjoyed it and then sent it to their friends . . . and so on. It wasn't long before it went viral.

Yes, Ginny Wheelright was intuitive about Ellen – not too bright.

11

Kentuckians howl with righteous indignation if outsiders refer to us as a violent, quarrelsome people . . . but we are. In fact, we are the only state in the nation with the dubious reputation to have assassinated our duly elected governor. On the sidewalk to the State Capitol of the morning of January 30, 1900, some Republicans decided that they didn't want a Democrat governor, so they shot the man instead. Who cares what the voters wanted.

But he got the last word – really. William Justus Goebel was sworn in as governor on his deathbed. But in the end, it didn't matter. Goebel died on February 3rd allegedly whispering these great words before the grim reaper took him, "Tell my friends to be brave, fearless and loyal to the common people."

Of course, everyone knows what Goebel really said after eating his last dinner of raw oysters was, "Doc, that was a damned bad oyster."

Doesn't have quite the same noble ring to it, does it?

Why bring up Goebel now?

I always say – if it walks like a duck, quacks like a duck, swims like a duck . . . it's a duck. You'll understand this comparison later in my tale of mayhem.

Besides, Goebel was late to his own funeral. Instead of the body going from Frankfort to Covington on the L&N line, the body had to be transported to Louisville, across the river to Indiana, then to Cincinnati, across the river again to Covington and then back the same route to Frankfort on the Queen and Crescent Railroad. The L&N owners hated Goebel and refused their service. Talk about petty.

Just as Goebel was late to his funeral, I was late to Addison DeWitt's.

Jake was having trouble finding a handicapped parking space. It seemed like all of Doreen's friends were infirm, so I got out and left Jake to park where he could. I wheeled my chair to the back of the memorial service for Addison DeWitt at the church on Market Street, hoping to be inconspicuous so I could snoop.

A couple of pews in front of me sat Detective Goetz, hoping to do the same. He was writing names in his worn out little notebook while I was sure someone else was taking down license plate numbers outside.

Hmmmmmm. Didn't Goetz tell me that he thought DeWitt's death was due to natural causes? Maybe the coroner had come up with a different view of things but I knew it was too soon for the report to be finished. What gives?

Up front sat Lady Elsmere, with Meriah and Matt behind Doreen who was making little whimpering noises as her daughter tried to comfort her. Lady Elsmere reached over the pew and sympathetically patted Doreen on the shoulder. Just like June. She so liked to be in the thick of things.

I must admit this was my first Episcopalian funeral. You know my views on the *Twenty-Third Psalm* at funerals. I was hoping against hope that it would not be repeated here. Oooops! I was wrong. A priest began reciting it.

I let out a long sigh, which was heard by Goetz, who swiveled around in his seat. Upon seeing me, he also let out a sigh.

Was that due to me?

He got up from his pew and sat beside me in a very uncomfortable stack chair. "Whaddya doing here?" he whispered.

"Why are you here?" I asked. "You said DeWitt's death was probably a heart attack. Coroner say differently?"

"See that girl crying in the corner over there?" replied Goetz. "I shouldn't be telling you this, but she has been hounding my office since DeWitt died and claiming that Mrs. DeWitt had something to do with his death."

"Really!!!!" I gave the young woman sobbing into her handkerchief a very good study. "Why are you telling me?"

"Because I don't want you poking your nose in this. If I tell you stuff, you have to keep it confidential and promise you won't go around stirring up things."

"What if I do tell someone?"

Goetz gave a very smarmy smile. "Then I'll arrest you for interfering. And I would, too; don't think I wouldn't."

"How about this? If I hear something interesting . . . now just listen . . . from my friends, let's say, then I tell you. It's quid pro quo. You tell me what's going on with O'nan. I know your department is keeping tabs on him somewhat."

Goetz's hound dog face looked thoughtful for a moment. "Okay. Information for information, but only if someone volunteers something – like at a dinner party. I don't want you to go around asking people questions, getting them all riled up."

"I will be a beacon of discretion. You just keep me informed about O'nan." I held out my pinky finger. "Pinky swear." Wiggling my finger, I demanded, "Pinky swear!"

The Detective looked around to see if anyone was watching and then wrapped his pinky with mine. We shook.

"By the way, who is the crying Madonna over there?"

"She says she was DeWitt's girlfriend and he was going to leave Mrs. DeWitt. Her name is Lacey Bridges."

"That's a motive for murder," I cautioned.

"Not if you read the prenup," replied Goetz. "DeWitt had no money. If he had left his wife for another woman, he would have walked out with just the clothes on his back."

"Maybe Doreen really loved him."

Goetz smiled. "Come on. Really? Always the romantic. That's what I like about you, Josiah. In many ways, you're an innocent. True love? What bull."

"So if he walked, Doreen would not have to give him any money," I said thoughtfully. "Maybe I'm right. She loved him and killed him in a fit of jealousy."

Goetz shook his head. "DeWitt bought two tickets to Venice for the following week."

"See there. He was running away with his girlfriend."

"Nope. He was taking Mrs. DeWitt on a second honeymoon. Made a big deal of it at the old lady's party. He wasn't about to leave his cozy nest."

"Maybe that was a cover for what he was really going to do, which was leave Doreen?"

"Doesn't fit. He initiated buying the airplane tickets. He was trying to keep his wife happy."

"So what are you going to do?"

"This is the last of the man-hours I can spare on this case. If something concrete doesn't show up soon, the case is going to be closed as death due to heart failure. There is no evidence to the contrary."

"I see."

"What?"

"I understand . . . it is just that the room felt so creepy.
I can't explain it but something besides a simple
heart attack was occurring. I understand, though, why
you might need to move on."

"Right. I can't use a 'creepy feeling' as evidence to
continue a case." With that last word, Goetz rose and
went outside.

I wanted to ask Goetz another question. Why were the
police called? When there is a medical emergency, 911 is
called for an ambulance. The police don't show up unless
there is foul play suspected and it's usually the paramedics
who call it in. But the paramedics and Officer Kelly
arrived about the same time – so who called the police . . .
and better yet – why? I made a mental note to find out.

Without me realizing it, the memorial service had
ended and people were starting to rise and meander down
the aisle. The priest announced the church had prepared
food and drink for the bereaved.

Things were looking up.

I waited for everyone to pass. Matt stopped by and
asked if he could wheel me but I shook my head. It was
easier for me to wait until after everyone else was settled.
I didn't like getting in the ambulatory folks' way. It was
rude.

Waiting at least ten minutes, I started for the food
when I heard, "Excuse me. Can I talk to you?"

I looked up and saw the young mourner for Addison.
She was looking bright-eyed and hopeful. "My name is
Lacey Bridges. Please, I need to talk with you, Mrs.
Reynolds."

"How do you know who I am?"

She gave a knowing look. "Oh come on. Everyone knows who you are."

"Really?"

"I don't mean to be impertinent, but I need to talk with you."

"About what?"

"The police won't listen. At least they won't listen to me." Lacey pulled a chair over so she was on eye level with me. "I know Doreen killed Addison. I just don't know how."

"Do you know why?"

Her young pretty face glowed with anticipation. She reminded me of a pretty Christmas tree before the limbs started to droop. "Yes, I do."

"Doreen killed him out of jealousy?"

"NO!" protested Lacey, frustrated. "She killed him because of greed."

"Greed?"

"This is what I can't get the police to understand. Doreen wanted to divorce Addison. She was tired of him but she couldn't divorce him because if she did, she would have to pay him a settlement if she filed without proof of abuse or adultery. That's why she hired me. She wanted me to seduce Addison and provide her with proof of adultery so she could divorce him without giving him a dime. It's all in the prenup."

"Your story is rather fantastic. What went wrong? You fall in love with Addison?"

"Yes, terribly. I wanted to marry him. I destroyed any evidence of him cheating and confronted Doreen about it."

"Did he know about Doreen hiring you?"

Lacey shook her head while wiping her dripping nose.

"Well, my dear, that is a cute story but there is one flaw. Addison had no intention of divorcing his wife. In fact, he was taking her on a trip to Venice to celebrate their marriage, a sort of second honeymoon. It was his idea and he bought the tickets."

"You're lying. He loved me. He was going to tell her."

"When the moment was right?"

Lacey nodded her head. The light streamed through the stained glass windows, giving her an ethereal glow.

Sighing, I said, "That right moment might have taken years. Men are notorious about not telling their wives about their mistresses . . . except for my husband. The actress Yvonne DeCarlo said, 'Men, no matter what their promises, rarely leave their spouses . . . the louses.' "

The young woman started backing away and pointed a finger at me. "He . . . he loved me. He was going to tell her. You're just like all the rest . . . trying to trip me up."

"Ask yourself this. If he had asked for a divorce, would he have received a settlement?"

"No," Lacey whispered.

"I'm sorry, young lady. He may have loved you, but he was not going to leave Doreen and her money anytime soon," I said, but I was talking to empty air. Lacey was gone. Somewhere a door slammed. I blew out a wad of air from my cheeks. Suddenly losing my appetite, I wheeled myself outside and called Jake from my cell phone. He'd parked down the street.

Within a moment, the car was in front of the church and Jake had a big grin on his face. He was happy to see me.

Oh Lord. Could I trust him? Would he break my heart like Lacey's was broken now?

Probably.

I would just have to stand it when the time came.

Before we headed home, we stopped at Franklin's apartment. He was not returning my calls and, frankly, I was very worried.

Jake knocked on the door while I waited in the car. Minutes passed but no one answered the door. Jumping over the porch railing, Jake headed for the back where he was going to break in. I waited tensely in the car praying, "Oh please Franklin, don't have done something stupid."

It seemed forever until the front door was opened by Franklin with Jake holding him up by his shirt collar. "Alright. Alright," hissed Franklin. "Let go, you big monkey."

I rolled down the car window. "You can be such a shit, Franklin, making me worry so."

"Come on in," said Franklin. "It is obvious that I can't keep you out."

An angry looking Jake pushed past Franklin and after opening the car door, picked me up and carried me into the house. Gently he placed me in one of Franklin's chintz chairs.

"Why haven't you returned my calls?"

Franklin plopped down in a chair across from me. "You know why. I needed time to lick my wounds."

"For what it's worth, I think Matt is making a big mistake," I replied.

"You think that. I think that. What do you think, Jake?"

"I think he should try this marriage with Meriah. It's more socially acceptable. He can have his own children. It's just less trouble over all."

"Oh, who in the hell asked you!" wailed Franklin.

"You did."

I turned around and gave Jake a big frown. Jake shrugged and retreated to the kitchen.

"What are you going to do, Franklin?" I asked.

Reaching into his pocket, Franklin pulled out a handkerchief and blew his nose. "I'm not going to become one of those screaming meanies who takes his business all over the streets. And I'm certainly not going to stay in town during the wedding."

"I see you have some bags packed by the door."

"I'm going on a long cruise. Josiah, I can't stay around here. I'll just fall apart. By the time I get back, I will have cried this all out. I am going to embarrass neither Matt nor myself by being hysterical, which is what I feel at the moment. Best I leave until I can contain myself."

"What did you say when Matt told you?"

"I was stunned. I thought, maybe another man, but marrying a woman and Meriah Caldwell on top of that? It just blew my mind. I told him he was making a mistake but that I wished him well. Then I asked him to leave."

Franklin blew his nose again. "You know what he said after that? He hoped we could stay friends. Friends! What a joke," Franklin sniffled.

"I tried to talk him out of marrying but Matt is determined."

Franklin folded his handkerchief and placed it back in his pocket. "Thank you for that. I just didn't want to see anyone. It's so humiliating. I mean . . . the money I have spent on bridal magazines would have paid for a car."

"You don't have to tell me."

"That's right. You got dumped too."

In the kitchen I heard Jake snicker.

"Is there anything I can do?" I asked, ignoring his remark.

Franklin looked at his watch. "Can you take me to the airport? My plane leaves in two hours. I might as well go to the airport now."

"Sure. No problem."

Jake gathered Franklin's luggage, and then me, into the car before we sped off to the Bluegrass Airport.

As Franklin was getting out of the car, he said, "I just keep thinking – why wasn't I enough? That ever cross your mind with Brannon?"

Before I could reply, Franklin sashayed through the doors. He didn't turn around to wave goodbye. When he thought we weren't looking, his head drooped.

I wondered if I was ever going to see Franklin again. And his words had struck deep. Why hadn't I been enough for Brannon? The nights I had lain awake wondering. I would never know.

Neither Jake nor I said a word all the way home.

12

I called Goetz early the next morning. Could I meet him for lunch?

"Show up at Hannah's on Lime at one o'clock," he said before hanging up.

That was good for me as I had a doctor's appointment before that. Some x-rays were taken and good luck seemed to be in my corner that morning. The Velcro cast was taken off. Jake had brought a sturdy medical cane as though he knew. Anyway, I felt relieved. I was tired of hearing Jake grunt when he picked me up and harp on the extra weight I needed to lose. I knew I needed to lose it. Geez, one thing at a time, okay, lover. Still it felt great to have that thing off me. The cast . . . not Jake.

Hmmm, I thought. Maybe we could get things grooving in the right direction now.

Jake and I got to Hannah's first and ordered lunch. I ordered for Goetz, knowing that he liked turkey sandwiches with mayo, chips, a crisp pickle and sweet iced tea. Don't ask me how I knew that, but I did.

A few minutes later, Goetz lumbered through the back door and upon seeing Jake, narrowed his eyes. "Jesus, can't you go anywhere without this guy hanging on?" muttered Goetz.

"Just sit down and behave," I replied, patting a seat.

The waitress brought out our food. Goetz didn't seem surprised that I had ordered for him. He took a huge bite out of the sandwich. "I was starving," he said, munching his food before taking a big gulp of tea. "Whadja need to see me for?"

"After Addison's memorial, Lacey Bridges talked to me."

"Yeah?"

"Told me a crazy story that Doreen *hired* her to seduce Addison so she could divorce him without giving him alimony. That's a motive for murder."

"Gave me the same. The problem is that there is no proof either way. There is a prenup that says Doreen has to have cause like abuse or adultery for a divorce; without it, she has to pay Addison a hefty sum."

"Well there," I said, slumping back in my seat. "That proves it."

"Proves nothing. Doreen has never talked to anyone about divorcing Addison . . . not her lawyer, not her daughter, no one. And there is no proof that Lacey Bridges ever had an affair with Addison DeWitt. There are no motel receipts, no love letters, no witnesses, nothing."

"She said she destroyed the proof."

"She must have done a good job because I can't find anything."

"Now why have you been looking? The medical examiner come back with something odd after you talked to me last?"

Goetz looked around the restaurant before leaning forward. "He had acetylsalicylic acid in his stomach."

"What's that?"

"The common aspirin," interjected Jake. "How much?"

"Not even a full tablet."

"So what?" I asked.

"Some people are very allergic to aspirin."

"Are you saying that Addison died from aspirin poisoning?"

"Looks that way."

"And that means murder?" I whispered, trying to wrap my mind around the news.

"Not necessarily," confided Goetz. "He could have complained of a headache and someone put an aspirin in his drink and just forgot to tell him, or he took half a pill thinking that such a small amount wouldn't harm him."

Jake wiped his mouth with a napkin. "I didn't hear him complain about anything like that. He was telling jokes and seemed fine one minute, and then the next he was having trouble breathing. Besides, if he were truly allergic, he wouldn't have taken any amount of aspirin. Too risky."

"Did he take a drink from a glass?" asked Goetz.

Jake shook his head. "Didn't really pay attention. I was listening to him plus some guy trying to sell me insurance. I don't remember him holding a glass; he was using his hands to tell his jokes."

"Did you have the glasses you took tested?"

Goetz nodded. "Nothing. This morning I went back to Lady Elsmere's with a warrant and took all the booze. I should get something back in a couple of days."

"I bet that went over well," I surmised, sorry that I had missed the confusion.

Goetz smiled. "She loved it. Lady Elsmere was practically jumping up and down. And that Meriah Caldwell. She was taking notes and following us around. It was creepy that two dames should find it such fun to have their house turned upside down."

"Those are two very bored women," confirmed Jake. "They like any diversion."

"Now what?" I asked.

"Wait," replied Goetz. "I've got some ideas to flush the truth out."

"Want to share?"

"Not at this time"

"Okay. Your turn," I said.

"O'nan is laying low. Waiting for the trial. We have an ankle bracelet on him. He is staying far away from you."

"How do you think the trial will go?"

Goetz patted my hand. "Don't worry."

"I wish I could be sure. I just don't trust that judge on the case."

Goetz's phone rang. He looked at it. "Gotta go," he said, taking out his wallet.

"I've got it covered," I said, waving his money away.

"Thanks." With that, Goetz strode out of the back of the restaurant without another word.

Jake watched him intently. "I don't trust that guy."

"Why do you say that?"

He patted his stomach. "I just feel it here."

"An icky feeling?"

"Yeah, real icky, baby."

I knew the "icks" feeling well.

WHEN BRANNON DIDN'T CALL

It had been three weeks since Brannon had left, and I hadn't heard a word from him. He wouldn't return my calls. Regardless of our marital meltdown, we had bills to pay for which we were both responsible.

So I took a deep breath and swung open the door to his architectural firm downtown, hoping to catch him in.

"Good morning, Betsy," I said to the receptionist, putting on a bright smile. "Is Brannon in?"

"Hello, goo . . . good morning," stuttered Betsy. For a moment she looked confused and started to reply until she thought better of it. Picking up the phone, she called one of Brannon's partners. "Wyman, Josiah is here looking for Brannon." Betsy glanced up at me and then spoke into the phone again. "I don't know. Yes, I will." She put the phone back on the hook. "Wyman will be right out. Would you like something to drink?"

"No, I just want to see Brannon. Is he here?" I could feel the heat rise on my face. Obviously Brannon had told the office that he didn't want to see me if I should pop in.

I was humiliated. My father had loaned Brannon the startup money for the firm. Regardless of what was occurring between us now, this was no way for Brannon to treat me . . . like a pariah. I wanted to break into tears but held my ground.

Wyman rushed out of his office. "Josiah, so good to see you," he said, holding out his hand.

I shook it. "I know you're busy, but I just wanted to speak with Brannon for a moment."

He gave Betsy a worried glance. "Well, that is a problem. Brannon's not here."

"I'll just wait in his office then until he comes back."

"Josiah, I think you'd better come into my office. I think there is a communication problem between you and Brannon."

I gave Wyman a weak smile. "Oh, you're starting to talk corporate BS, so there must be a hiccup somewhere."

He smiled back and pulled at my arm gently. "Please, Josiah. We need to talk."

I followed Wyman into his office, dreading what he was going to say to me. He pulled out a chair for me and then pulled one up for himself.

"You looked surprised to see me, Wyman."

"I'll be honest – I am. What has Brannon told you?"

"That's just it. Brannon walked out three weeks ago and I haven't heard from him since. I came here to see him about bills we need to pay."

Wyman look embarrassed.

"I'm sorry to be so blunt, but there it is. He's left me." I folded my hands in my lap.

"And you have no idea where he is?"

"None. Wyman, what is going on?"

"Josiah, I don't know how to tell you this, but Brannon is no longer with the firm. Jess and I bought him out at – at his insistence – six months ago."

"What?"

"He said he needed money to pay for Asa's legal bills and demanded that we buy him out. Under our contract, we had no choice but to comply."

I sat silent in my chair.

"You had no idea?"

I shook my head, tears threatening to spill down my face. Wyman handed me his monogrammed handkerchief. "I mortgaged the Butterfly to pay for Asa's legal fees. Brannon hasn't contributed a dime to paying them off."

Wyman looked at his hands rather than at my bereaved face. He didn't like it when women cried in his presence. He felt a compulsion to make them feel better, but was damned if he knew what to do in this situation. How do you make a woman feel better when she finds out that her husband is hiding money from her and has been lying for over six months?

"How much did he ask for?"

"Half a million."

"Half a million!!! Good Lord." I was silent for a while, taking it all in. "What else do you know? Do you know why he wanted out?"

Wyman tugged at his collar. "Not really."

"Wyman, don't you lie to me. We go back a long time. I need to know what's going on."

"Jo, he had been acting funny for over a year. At first I thought it was just a middle-age crisis and would blow over, but it just kept going on. He wasn't himself. Brannon was moody and withdrawn. He did his job, but he started complaining about the hours he had to put in."

"Did he say anything about Asa?"

"He was resentful. He felt that Asa's situation had cost the firm jobs, but then would complain about the long hours. It didn't make sense."

"He and Asa were always so close, but after she was arrested, he barely spoke to her. Brannon was not there for her."

"He was not the Brannon that we knew for years, that's for sure."

"Do you think that Asa's situation put too much strain on him?"

"It put some but not all. This was going on before Asa got arrested."

"I think you're right. He has seemed restless for a long time. Do you know where he is, Wyman?"

"Aw, Josiah." Wyman reared back in his chair.

"Come on. Give. I think you know where he is."

"I don't want to get in the middle of this."

"You are in the middle of this, man. Tell me. Where is Brannon?"

Wyman's Southern patrician looks twisted as he spoke. He liked Josiah and didn't want to hurt her. And this was going to hurt like hell. "It is rumored that he is living in the guest house of Ellen Boudreaux."

13

I was sitting in the living room, reading the *Herald-Leader* when I heard the front door being unlocked and someone punching in the alarm code. Before I could call for Jake, Asa strode into the room.

"Well, it's about time," I cried, giving my cheek up for a kiss. "I called such a long time ago. Where have you been?"

Asa threw her gloves on the end table before plopping down on the couch. "I have been working on your behalf."

"Stirring up trouble?"

Asa grinned. "Let's say I've been muddying the water."

"Ellen is making accusations that you stole into her house and robbed her."

"Is she now?"

"Did you?"

"Mother, you know that if you have knowledge of a crime, that makes you an accessory after the fact."

"Jumping Jehosaphat. Does that mean yes?"

"Change the subject, please. I understand from Jake that Matt is leaping into matrimony . . . with a woman yet."

"That's not all." It took me the greater part of an hour to tell her about the Addison DeWitt case.

"So you are Goetz's spy?"

I reared up. "That's such a nasty word. People tell me things. I relay that info to him and he keeps me informed about what O'nan is doing."

"Does he really? You think you can trust Goetz?"

"Why not?"

"Just wondering out loud."

I gave Asa a curious look. "Are you holding something back from me?"

"Please don't grill me. I just got home. I want to take a bath and then a nap."

"You're evading me."

"I swear that after dinner I will tell you about the naughty things I have been up to."

The front door opened and Jake walked in. He blanched when he saw Asa.

She gave him a sour look.

"I didn't see a car outside."

"I had my driver let me out."

"I was just doing my perimeter rounds."

"And you didn't hear a car on a gravel driveway?"

"No ma'am."

"Perhaps you should have your hearing checked?"

"Yes ma'am."

I interrupted what I could tell was the beginning of a scolding. "Jake, why don't we barbeque out tonight. It's such a pretty evening. Let's get out those steaks we got from the Farmers' Market."

Asa rose from her chair. "I am going to take a nap. Wake me when dinner is ready."

"Of course, dear."

Asa gave me a kiss before she left the room. Jake gazed after her.

I couldn't tell what he was thinking but thought I should leave him to his thoughts. "I think I will follow suit, Jake."

"I think that is a good idea, baby. Take a nap so you'll be fresh for dinner."

Without the Velcro cast, my usual limp was less pronounced, so I got out of the chair and into my bedroom on my own. It was a small accomplishment, but it made me feel good. It wasn't long before I fell into Morpheus' arms.

*

I awoke to find Baby's snout in my face. He licked my nose, knowing that it would get me out of bed. I stumbled into the bathroom, washed my face, washed my arms, brushed my teeth, changed my underwear and combed my hair. After putting on a fresh caftan, I made

my way to the patio where Jake had steaks on the grill.
Asa was setting the table for dinner.

"That smells wonderful," I complimented, peering over
Jake's shoulder at the grill where steak and shrimp sizzled
along with sweet peppers, onions and potatoes.

"Mom, what do you want to drink?" Asa asked on her
way into the house.

"Just some tea, dear. I'm not allowed anything else," I
said, mugging a look at Jake. I quickly patted Jake on the
fanny before finding a seat.

Asa came back out with tea and wine. Just moments
after she'd filled everyone's glasses, Jake put platters of
food on the table. Asa let out a gleeful sound. "You
know how much a dinner like this would cost in New
York?" she said.

"How much?"

"Too much, Mom."

"Then maybe it's time for you to relocate. Maybe
come home."

Asa hesitated before she spoke. "I am thinking of
relocating . . . but to London."

I put down my fork. "What?"

"It won't be until next year, but I feel that I have to
make this move for the company's sake."

"Why?"

"It's closer to where most of my people are working
and it will be less expensive in the long run to have the
company centered in London for the next couple of
years."

"What about your apartment in New York?"

"I'm going to keep it. I had a key made for you. You use it."

There was a long silence at the table before I started eating again. "It's not forever?"

"No, just a couple of years and then my contract runs out. I don't want to renew it again. I'll be pulling out then. I'd rather investigate insurance fraud like art thefts than what I'm doing now. It's an easier way to make a living."

"So you are in Afghanistan," I stated matter of factly.

Asa didn't reply but instead nibbled on a shrimp.

"Please, Mother, understand."

"I do. I do. It's your life."

"Thanks, Mom."

I smiled weakly. What else could I do? Asa had made her choice.

"A few weeks in New York doesn't sound bad, does it, Josiah?" asked Jake, trying to put a positive spin on Asa's revelation.

"No, it doesn't."

"We could take in a few shows, eat at expensive restaurants, go to museums. Maybe even take Franklin with us so the two of you could go shopping."

"Yes, that would be fun."

"Two years will go like that," Jake said, snapping his fingers. "You'll be busy. You'll see."

Asa gave Jake a grateful look before cutting into her steak.

One of the kittens, now almost full grown, jumped on the table. I put her wiggling body down on the ground.

Before giving me a malevolent look, she went over to Baby's bowl and started to eat out of it. Her siblings joined her. None of the kittens trusted me anymore since I'd had them fixed, but I just couldn't let them run around like promiscuous minxes.

The only animal I wanted having sex on this farm in the near future was me. And now I was determined that was going to happen. I was going to go on with my life.

If Asa wanted to throw her life away on military contracts, I was not going to light a candle in the window and wait for her to come home. I was going to put some miles on my carriage before the wheels rusted off. It was time to join the dance of life again.

14

Something woke me.

It was Baby's growls as he peered out the bedroom's patio door. With the moonlight spilling into the room, I could see that the kittens were with him. Several perched on his back looking out the glass door as the others tussled for a spot around the mastiff's legs.

"What is it, Baby?"

The fawn mastiff turned his blind eye towards me and shook his head a little as if to say "danger." He turned back to the glass, emitting a low threatening growl.

The motion lights around the pool came on.

"Jake!" I hissed. "Jake."

Climbing out of bed, I reached for my wolf's head cane and stumbled to the bedroom door. It was locked. Jake must have locked me in and gone searching the grounds. I looked through a secret peephole Jake had installed for me. The hallway was dark.

Limping into the closet, I searched through my shoeboxes until I found both my stun gun and handgun.

I no longer kept them near my bed, as the animals were always scampering around looking for a place to nestle.

After checking the safety, I placed the handgun on my dresser where I hunkered down beside it with the phone, walkie-talkie and stun gun. If someone came through either the patio or the steel doors, I could get off a good shot at them. If I missed, their shot would go over my head, as I was low, giving me another opportunity.

I didn't dare call Jake on the walkie-talkie as it might give away his position. He was outside somewhere. I strained to listen, as did the animals.

A large shadow fell across the patio door. I gasped. Someone was outside my patio door. Oh Lord, where was Jake? Where was Asa?

Baby began barking, rearing up against the glass door. Flicks of foam escaped from his mouth as he frantically pawed the glass. The cats scampered under the bed and were no more to be seen.

BANG!!!!! A chair was thrown against the patio door, creating a huge noise against the house.

I didn't scream. My hands were shaking badly as I raised the stun gun, while the other reached for the handgun, placing it beside me on the floor.

The hit against the house had set off the alarm. It wouldn't be long before someone came, but a lot could still happen before the law arrived.

Then there was a shout followed by a crashing noise. And a gunshot.

Now silence.

Except for Baby.

I strained to listen. "Baby, shut up. I can't hear."

Baby looked at me with disdain and kept threatening the intruder with his loud barks and growls.

The silence continued. The shadow did not reappear. Baby stopped growling and then commenced to adjust his head so he could see better out of his one good eye. He thumped over, snorted snot on me and took his position back on the patio door, satisfied that I was safe.

I wiped the gooey stuff on my nightgown. For some reason, Baby's goo took my fear away. Should I unlock the door and look for Asa and Jake? What if they were injured? Was someone still out there? Had they found a way into the house?

Suddenly the alarm went off. Someone thudded down the hallway.

"Josiah, unlock the door. It's Jake."

My heart leaped. "I can't. Baby's too wild. I'm afraid he might attack you."

"Okay. Stay in your room then. Don't unlock the door until I come for you."

I made my way to the door and pressed my lips against it. "Are you alright? Asa?"

"We're both fine. You?"

"Scared. What happened?"

"Will tell you later. I'm going to check on the barns now."

"No, Jake. Don't leave me. Please."

"You'll be fine. Just call me on the walkie-talkie if you need me."

I didn't want to be left alone. Still I said, "Okay."

"Remember. Stay locked in until I come for you."

I nodded my head.

"Josiah?"

"Yes. I will wait for you." Pressing my ear against the door, I heard Jake retreat down the hallway.

Much to Baby's chagrin, I pulled the draperies closed. But I made it up to him when I pulled out a pint of ice cream from my little freezer and gave it to him. It was the least I could do for his gallant protection. I rubbed his head as he lapped up the ice cream.

Sensing someone was eating something they were not, the cats stuck their heads out from beneath my Hans Weger bed. They looked at me with total dismay. Chuckling, I got out another pint of ice cream and spooned it onto the floor. I would clean up the mess later.

Realizing that I was still in the dark, I turned on the lights, tinkled, brushed my hair, brushed my teeth, washed my face and my nether regions as I had . . . you get the idea. I changed into sweatpants and top, then sat at my dresser waiting.

It seemed like an eternity before voices sounded in the hallway. I looked through the peephole. Lights throughout the house were turned on. Jake strode down the hallway, knocking on the door. "Josiah, it's me. Unlock the door."

"Anyone with you?"

"Yeah. Charles and a cop."

"I'm going to let Baby out. Everyone should stand very still until Baby checks them out. I won't be able to hold him. He's too wound up."

"We're ready. Let him out. I've got a leash."

I slowly opened the door, giving Baby ample room to rush out. I didn't want my 225-pound guard dog to knock me down in his excitement. Baby quickly smelled Jake and started to pound past him when Jake grabbed his collar and attached a leash. Baby turned and snapped at Jake. Taking the other end of the leash, Jake tapped Baby's nose and commanded him to sit. Baby snarled. Jake jerked on the leash and commanded again, this time straddling Baby. Seeing that he was dominated by an Alpha, Baby finally gave in.

Jake rubbed the dog's ears and gave him a biscuit treat.

I pushed past them and went into the great room where Charles and a cop were waiting. The cop's eyes grew very big at the sight of Baby following me.

"Just stand still and let him smell you," I cautioned. "He's scared and not very well trained. Oh dear, I guess I shouldn't have said that."

Charles held out his hand for Baby to sniff. Recognizing Charles' scent, Baby thundered past to the cop.

"Don't worry. I've got a good hold on him," reassured Jake. "Just hold out your hand and talk to him."

"You sure he's not gonna bite me?"

"Mastiffs rarely bite. They knock people down and sit on them. I'm not kidding. This breed is several thousand years old. Julius Caesar brought them back from England to fight in the circuses. Knights took these dogs with them on the Crusades." Jake rubbed Baby's scarred head. "He comes from a noble lineage. A warrior race of dogs."

The young cop reluctantly held out his hand. Baby sniffed him, gave him a curious glance with his good eye and snapped up another treat that Jake gave him. Seeing Baby's haunches had relaxed, Jake let him go. Immediately Baby stuck his snout in the policeman's crotch.

I pulled Baby away, mumbling an apology. I threw a chew toy into a corner where Baby retrieved it and laid down, but not before circling three times. Why do dogs do that?

The cop audibly breathed again and sat down where I motioned. Charles followed suit.

Hearing the front door open and close, we looked up as Asa strolled in. She was covered in soot and smelled like a chimney. I noticed then that Charles was filthy too. He took out a handkerchief and wiped his face.

Leaving for a moment, Jake came back with water bottles and hot wet washcloths. They were gratefully accepted.

"What happened?" I asked.

We looked to Charles to do the explaining. "Some crazy woman tried to burn down one of the horse barns!"

"Is everyone alright?" I asked, alarmed. Barn burning was a very serious and horrible thing to witness.

"We got everyone and all the horses out of all the barns. Not a scratch on them."

I looked at Asa and Jake.

"Everything is fine at our place," replied Asa. Jake and I have doubled checked all the animals and hives. They are fine."

"Someone threw a chair at my patio door and I heard a scuffle."

Glancing at his dirty washcloth, Charles stated, "That was Jake and this boy, Officer Snow, tackling that crazy woman. Snow and I had chased her across my land onto your property till we met up with her here. Didn't you hear the fight?"

"Yes, I did," I replied, ashamed of my own cowardice when everyone else had been outside trying to put out the fires – literally. "Who was she?"

Office Snow looked up. "She said her name was Lacey Bridges. She was rambling about some story that Lady Elsmere was using her influence to hide a murder at her house and stuff like that."

I looked hard at Snow. He looked familiar. "Do I know you?"

Turning red, Officer Snow replied, "Yes ma'am. I sat in your driveway for weeks this past summer. You gave me some vegetables one time."

It was my turn to feel heat rise on my face. "Of course, Officer Snow. Sorry I forgot." Trying to change the subject, I offered, "I know this Lacey Bridges. She approached me at Addison DeWitt's funeral. She claimed to have been Addison's girlfriend and that he was going to leave Doreen but that Doreen killed him. The reason why Doreen would murder her husband was rather confusing. Anyway, she wanted me to help convince the police that Doreen was behind Addison's death. Where is she now?"

"She's on her way to jail," responded Officer Snow. "In the morning, she'll go before a judge. She will most probably be turned over for a psych evaluation."

"So she was burning down the barn in protest?" I asked again.

Charles looked tired and sad. "It seems so. Just plain mean, if you ask me." He looked at his watch. "I gotta go. See you folks later on tomorrow. Lady Elsmere is waiting for me."

Asa rose and escorted Charles out. She was fond of Charles and thought of him as an uncle. Asa had known him all her life. Charles was one of the few people that had believed her story when she had been hounded out of Washington.

I realized then that Matt was missing. "Where's Matt?" I asked, holding my breath that nothing had happened to him.

"It was Matt who called the fire department. He said he awoke for some reason and looked out the back window and saw flames coming out of the barn. He called me and I woke up Asa. We rushed over to help.

He's with Meriah now. I think Matt will stay at the big house the rest of the night."

"That's good," I replied.

"You were never in danger," said Jake. "I made sure."

Smiling, I said, "I know that. I was just of no help at all though."

"Your time will come again, Mom. Just keep getting better," encouraged Asa, coming back in the room.

I patted her arm.

She yawned. "I'm going to take a shower, get this stink off me and then go back to bed. This has been too much excitement for me."

"Same here," concurred Jake.

I took my cue. "I'm going back to bed also. See you both in the morning." Realizing that I wouldn't see Jake again until breakfast, as he stayed in his own room when Asa was home, I padded off to bed with Baby.

Darn!

15

Mike Connors and I looked at what was left of the barn – not much. Smoke was still rising from some of the fallen beams. I shuddered. A barnburner. It reminded me of the movie *The Long Hot Summer* with Paul Newman playing Ben Quick. In the countryside, a barnburner was almost akin to a murderer.

Firemen and the insurance investigator were in the ruins poking around and taking readings.

Finally the Fire Chief conferred with some of his men and stepped out of the charred wood and over to Connors. He looked dubiously at me.

"What started the fire?" asked Connors.

"Just like the lady told us last night," grumbled the Chief. "She started it with gasoline in the back."

"It's a wonder all the horses got out," I marveled.

"She stated that she let all the horses out before she set the fire," replied the Chief.

"Those horses are very high-spirited and hard to handle. I don't think one woman could have gotten all those horses out."

"You got them accounted for?" asked the Chief. Connor nodded.

The Chief shrugged. "A determined person can do almost anything, if she's got her mind turned to it." He looked to me for confirmation.

"You sure she didn't have help?" asked Connor.

"Nothing to indicate that," replied the Chief. "Everything will be in my report. Even the recommendation last year when I told you to put in a new water line to the barn complex. There is not enough water pumping through now. What if she had set two barns on fire, especially the one with the mares and foals? That would had been a tragedy for sure, Mike."

Mike threw up his hands. "I know. I know. I just didn't expect someone to set fire to the place."

"This all started with Addison's death," I interjected. "Chain reaction. No one could have foreseen these events."

The Chief patted Mike on the back. "Don't mean to be so hard on you, Mike. All the facts will be in my report."

"I know that you're doing your job. I'm just mad at myself for not doing mine," groused Mike before stumping off.

Giving the Chief a brief nod, I started the motor in my golf cart and headed back to the Butterfly when I spied Shaneika with Comanche strolling over to Lady Elsmere's track. Her trainer and Velvet Maddox were with her. A rider was atop Comanche. I went to intercept them.

"Are you sure you want to train today?" I asked, riding along side them walking.

Shaneika shot a look at Miss Velvet.

"Comanche is totally oblivious to the commotion," stated Miss Velvet. "He is a true narcissist. If it doesn't interfere with his feeding or safety, he could care less."

We got to the track and a prancing Comanche entered it. Everyone else took places around the railing. The trainer took out a stopwatch and cried, "Go!"

Comanche took off in his usual lackadaisical gallop.

Shaneika turned to Miss Velvet. "Are you sure this is going to work?"

"Not sure of anything," said Miss Velvet. "But that horse won't do nothing if it is not in his interest to do so. That's why you're going to give him a treat if he comes round that bend running like the Devil is after him." She pulled Shaneika over to the railing and instructed, "Now when he comes round the last bend, you hold out your arm real far and let him see that peppermint. He's got to see it."

"You think a peppermint is going to inspire that lump of meat to win a race?" I snorted.

"Hush," commanded Miss Velvet. "That horse loves only two things, his companion goats 'cause they look up to him and peppermint."

I rolled my eyes and shot a look at Shaneika but she was earnestly watching for Comanche. When Comanche came round the bend, Shaneika leaned over the railing and waved the bag of red and white candies.

It didn't seem like anything had changed but then Comanche thundered past us, depositing little bits of the turf on our heads.

The trainer stopped the clock. Miss Velvet and Shaneika bent over to take a look at it.

"Well, I'll be," said the trainer. "Four seconds better. He wouldn't win a race still, but this is the best time he's ever had."

Miss Velvet gave me a smug look. "Now, honey, you give him some peppermint right now and tell him if he does better tomorrow, you will give him more peppermint. Make him understand that the faster he goes, the more peppermint he will get. He has to earn it. No more free treats. Go on now. Tell him," coached Miss Velvet pushing Shaneika towards the sweating horse.

Shaneika stole a glance at me before telling Comanche in a no-nonsense voice that she expected him to work like the rest of us and that he would only get peppermint if he kept increasing his speed. She also went into length about how she would have to sell him if he didn't start doing better at races because she couldn't afford him.

Comanche gave her a wide eyeball stare before snorting and pawing the ground.

"He understands," said Miss Velvet. "He'll do better. My work is done here. I'll send you a bill after he wins his first race."

"That's all?" asked Shaneika.

"Horses aren't that complicated. He'll work for sweets. If I thought for one moment that you would sell him for horse meat, I wouldn't help you." Velvet Maddox smiled. "But I can tell you love him." Always one to have the last word, Miss Velvet strode back to the barn where she'd left her big farm truck.

Shaneika looked at me and shrugged. Could it be that simple?

Comanche winning a race for peppermints?

There is a first for everything . . . I guess.

16

Lady Elsmere agreed. It was time to have a little talk with Doreen Doris Mayfield DeWitt.

"But we shouldn't spook her," I cautioned.

Lady Elsmere took a sip of her tea, lost in thought. Her ruby and diamond bracelet clanged against the fine china cup.

"I know," chirped Meriah. "My book is being released at Morris Book Shop in several days. Why don't I ask her personally to come?"

"Is that the book about me?" I huffed.

"No, silly. Just someone who resembles you," Meriah pouted. "Now don't spoil this book for me. It's a good mystery and the heroine will do you justice."

"Is she good looking?" I asked.

"Stunning!"

"Okay," I said sarcastically. "As long as I look good."

"I will call Doreen," declared Lady Elsmere, "and ask her to come. She knows me better. I know for a fact that she's going to Florida after Matt and Meriah's wedding."

"Then we all three can approach her at different times and ask her questions," said Meriah, looking very pleased. Instead of writing about solving murders, she was actually investigating one. What a great story this would make for her Hollywood friends.

"I will write down a list of questions that should be asked," I directed, "and then we can divide them. Now, you realize that you just can't blurt them out. They need to be asked with some finesse."

"Really!" sputtered June. "You'd think you were the only one in the room with some sophistication."

"I'm just saying that if she did indeed murder her husband, then she might react in a negative fashion – like, oh, I don't know, maybe trying to knock us off too."

"Don't be so dramatic," rejoined June, turning towards Meriah. "She's always such a drama queen."

I threw up my hands.

Meriah had the grace to look sheepish. "She did fall off a cliff trying to solve a murder," she replied, coming to my defense.

"That was only because Josiah was too fat to outrun that nasty policeman."

Looking amused, I said, "and how do you think you are going to get away from nasty Doreen when you are older than Methuselah, you old bat?"

"Charm, my dear, charm," answered Lady Elsmere, taking a sip of her tea.

Shaking my head, I wrote down a series of questions and gave sections to Lady Elsmere and Meriah.

After discussing the subtle ways of interrogating Doreen without her getting wise to us, I took my leave of the lady of the manor and her court jester.

I called Jake and told him I was heading home. It was his protocol that he liked to be waiting for me.

When I arrived home, he was on his cell phone looking very disturbed. I couldn't hear what he was saying due to the thunder of the waterfalls coming from the fluted gutter of the Butterfly's second roof. Jake's face was flushed and his expression was one of formulating an opinion on something foul. He looked like he had just been given something rotten to eat.

I wanted to ask him who he had been talking to but didn't.

He acted aloof all evening, just giving grunts when I talked to him.

Hearing him take a shower later that evening, I quietly entered his room. Finding his cell phone, I pushed the buttons to see where his calls had originated. His last call was from a Pauline Dosh.

I felt the ground move beneath my feet.

Pauline was the name of his ex-wife.

Putting the phone back, I went to my room. I rummaged around until finding my best negligee. I combed my hair and put on some blush. Then I sat at my dressing table waiting for Jake.

Seeming like forever, he finally strode into the room. Seeing me, Jake stopped short and gave a questioning look.

I went over and locked him in my arms. "It's time, Jacob," I whispered. I tilted my head up and caressed his lips with mine. And then it began.

Jake picked me up and carried me to the bed.

17

I was at my booth at the Farmers' Market selling my honey when Doreen suddenly popped up. She was wearing a lemon-colored jumpsuit. She looked like a walking banana. It played hell with her florid complexion.

"Hello," she said, pulling a bottle of clover honey off the table and into her canvas bag.

"Hello, Doreen," I replied. "I'm surprised to see you here."

We shook hands. She had already switched her wedding ring to her widow hand and had placed the rocks to underside of her finger, causing them to dig into my skin when we clasped hands. That was okay if she wanted to play dirty. I dug my fingernails into her flesh and didn't flinch until she released my hand.

What a little bitch. I've met women like her before who "accidentally" step on your foot or give you a cut while handing you paper and then apologize profusely. Nothing is worse than a paper cut.

Doreen gave me a distasteful smile.

I gave her one back. No way was I going to check the damage on my hand with her around. She must have thought the same thing, as she didn't check her palm either. I felt smug as I saw a little blood on her hand. Served her right.

Doreen handed me eight dollars.

I put the money in my change box.

On her left hand, Doreen was wearing a large gold button ring. It had brushed my skin when I reached for the money. I remembered she had been wearing it the night of the party.

"Interesting ring," I mentioned. "May I try it on?"

"I'd rather not. I'm fastidious about my jewelry." She gave me a lopsided grin. "I got this in Italy. Very unusual, don't you think?"

Why was this woman trying to piss me off?

"Yes," I replied, observing it carefully. "You know it reminds me of something but I can't quite put my finger on it. When were you in Italy?"

"Oh, years ago," said Doreen. "During my first marriage." Doreen looked around sheepishly.

I stretched my neck to see what she was looking for.

Doreen laughed again. "I've got some idiot stalking me. She claims that Addison was seeing her but I know for a fact that he was not. She's in a psych hospital for burning something down. Something about being delusional. But I still look for her. Better safe than sorry, right?"

"Lacey Bridges?"

"Yes! How did you know?"

"She approached me at Addison's funeral, and tried to convince the police that you killed Addison."

Doreen gave a brittle laugh. It came off as phony.

"You didn't, did you?"

"What?"

"Kill Addison."

"Silly girl," answered Doreen. "Now why would I want to kill my own husband?"

"Lacey claims that you were tired of him and wanted to get rid of him, but couldn't because the prenup states that if you filed for divorce, Addison would get a large settlement."

"But I could if he was having an affair, is that what you're saying?"

"You would have to prove adultery to the judge first. That's why she says you hired her to seduce Addison and provide you with evidence."

"If that were true, why didn't it happen?"

"Because she fell in love with him."

Doreen snorted a short laugh. Sounded like a hyena this time.

"Oh, Josiah, I heard that you had a head for strange stories, but this takes the cake."

"Then why do you think she's following you?"

"Because she's a nut. Didn't you have someone harassing you who's a nut? Don't you use a cane because of an obsessive person still making your life miserable?"

"Touché."

Doreen leaned over the table. "Let's not butt heads. I really came down here wanting to thank you for coming to Addison's funeral. I saw that you were alone and with the difficulty you have in walking – well, I just wanted to thank you."

"I liked Addison," I replied.

"I wonder if you would do me a favor?" asked Doreen, pushing her silver blond hair back. "If that woman contacts you again, if she ever gets out . . . will you let me know?"

"Sure. No problem, but wouldn't the police let you know?" I knew the real reason Doreen was here. She had seen me talking to Lacey Bridges at the funeral and wanted to know what was said. That made sense to me.

"The police have mix-ups, now don't they." Doreen looked around again before moving off.

I started to say something, but was cut off by another customer who wanted to pay me. It was then, out of the corner of my eye, that I saw Lacey Bridges across the street watching us. It gave me the chills.

So Lacey Bridges was out and stalking Doreen again. I called out to Doreen to tell her but she had disappeared into the crowd.

I phoned Jake, who was milling around the Market somewhere, and asked him to come to my booth. I didn't want to be alone. Within a minute, Jake was at the booth, listening to my tale. When I finished, he motioned to the

Market Manager and related that the Market had a possible stalker. The Manager called security and put his staff on alert.

Jake also called Detective Goetz and told him.

Goetz promised that he would look up to see whether Doreen had a restraining order against Lacey Bridges. He would also inform the DA.

I breathed a sign of relief. I didn't have to worry any more about crazy stalkers that day.

It turned out later that I was wrong, but how was I supposed to know that fate would take hold?

18

I kept thinking about Doreen's ring. It sort of rang a bell with me. No pun intended.

On a hunch, I pulled out my books on Renaissance paintings and looked in the glossaries for mention of the notorious Borgia family. Finally I found a reference to Dosso Dossi for his painting *Portrait Of A Youth* painted in 1514. Flipping to the correct page, there was the picture of a golden-haired youth dressed in dour clothing, almost like a Puritan's of the seventeenth century instead of the flamboyant, rich clothing of Rome during the flowering of the Renaissance. It was also hard to tell if the youth was male or female even though the print stated that person was Lucrezia Borgia.

I had seen several portraits of Lucrezia during my travels to Italy and this person did resemble that young girl.

Lucrezia Borgia was the illegitimate daughter of Rodrigo Borgia, also known as Pope Alexander VI. The corrupt political and sexual machinations of Pope Alexander VI, which included the famous Chestnut Ball at the Vatican, are said to have laid the groundwork for the Reformation in 1520. Among the many juicy accusations against the Borgia family was incest between father and daughter, orgies and most particularly – political assassinations by poison. Nice family, huh.

It was rumored that Lucrezia did her fair share of poisoning by use of a special ring with a secret compartment filled with poison, which she used on selected guests during dinner.

And, looking at the portrait I saw a ring on her finger – a large gold bauble just like Doreen was wearing. Was Doreen's copy of Lucrezia Borgia's ring hollow too? Did it have a special compartment?

That's what I needed to find out. I drummed the desk. Now how could I get that ring off Doreen's finger to see?

I would figure a way.

19

The bookstore was packed. I managed to grab a seat in the back near the bathroom. Jake stood in a corner watching everyone. I kept mouthing for him to smile but he was miserable at functions like this. He hated small talk and confined spaces where he couldn't control the traffic. This was Jake's idea of a tactical nightmare.

What was one person's hell was heaven for another. Lady Elsmere pushed her way back and sat in the seat I had saved for her. "Isn't this grand!" she purred. "Meriah's book is going to be a big hit."

"Oooo," I cried. "Someone just stepped on my foot." Indeed there was someone standing in front of me with her fanny in my face. I grabbed my ebony cane and was about to insert the wolf's head into an orifice when Jake asked the lady to move, which she did. Jake went back to his corner seemingly happier and I had some breathing space in front of me.

"I'm not going to stay if this crowd keeps up," I whispered to Lady Elsmere. "There is no way we can have a conversation with Doreen under these conditions." I looked up towards the door and saw Matt waving at me. He seemed very relaxed and happy. I waved back.

Before Lady Elsmere could answer, Meriah was pushing her way through with Doreen in tow. "Look who I found," giggled Meriah, grabbing a chair. She pushed a confused Doreen into it. "Now you girls have fun. I've got to sign books. Great turnout, huh?"

Doreen turned to look at us with suspecting eyes. "My, this place is packed. One can hardly get a breath."

"That's why we're hiding back here," confided Lady Elsmere.

I nodded in agreement.

Lady Elsmere plowed right in. "Doreen, did you hear that someone tried to burn down my horse barns?"

Doreen blinked. "Yes. That's terrible."

"I think it was some woman who has a connection to you."

Squirming in her chair, Doreen answered, "I have been having trouble with a stalker. It might be the same woman."

"Her name is Lacey Bridges," stated Lady Elsmere.

"Yes, that's her name, but I've nothing to do with her.
I have never met this woman, but she keeps going to
the police and telling them that I murdered Addison. She
is making my life miserable."

"So sorry to hear that. It's awful that innocent folk
have to deal with people with mental health issues like
that. Back in the day, we just locked them up and didn't
have to bother with them."

Everyone who lives here knows that is a lie. We don't
lock up our crazies. We have them run for political office
or become grand marshals at the Fourth of July parades.
I stifled a laugh, but said nothing. This was Lady
Elsmere's party.

"That right," agreed Doreen, nodding her head. "I'm
afraid every time I go out, but now she is under
observation, isn't she?"

"That's not what I understand," I replied. Hadn't
Goetz called her about Bridges?

Doreen ignored me. "As soon as Meriah's wedding is
over, I'm going to Florida and put this all behind me."

"Really?"

"Yes, I'm going to sell the house and leave Kentucky
for good."

"Oh, surely you will want to keep your beautiful
home?" questioned Lady Elsmere.

"There are beautiful houses in Florida and my daughter
is going to join me. We are going to start over."

"I think that is the best thing," I commiserated. "Start
over. Where will you be locating to?"

"Florida," answered Doreen impatiently.

"But where in Florida?" I asked.

"On the gulf side," dodged Doreen.

"I hope you'll be happy," interrupted Lady Elsmere. "Let's change the subject. I want to show you my new antique cameo I'm wearing. I just bought it a couple of days ago." She took off the pin and handed it to Doreen. "Look at this, Doreen. It opens and has a secret compartment."

Doreen held the brooch up the light, admiring it. "Fascinating."

"And that's a lovely ring you have," exclaimed Lady Elsmere pointing at Doreen's ring. "May I see it?"

Doreen blanched. I could tell she was looking for a way to refuse. "I don't think I can get it off."

"Oh, sure you can," I said. "Just give it a good tug." I reached for her hand, which she pulled away.

Seeing that there was no graceful way to decline, Doreen reluctantly pulled off the ring and handed it to Lady Elsmere.

Smiling, Lady Elsmere tried on the ring. "People used to keep hair locks of the deceased in my brooch. That's what it was made for."

"I see," said Doreen. She handed the brooch back.

Lady Elsmere began taking off the ring but seemed to be having trouble. She fussed with it until, "My goodness. Doreen, your ring opens. Did you know it did that?"

Lady Elsmere and I peered closer at the now opened ring.

"Yes, I did," replied Doreen, trying to hide her anger. She closed the ring and put it on her finger.

"What do you think the ring was used for?" I asked.

"Women used to keep their snuff in rings like this," replied Doreen.

"I didn't know that. I though they used special snuff boxes," I replied.

"They also used rings as well. I got this in Italy, remember. Lots of women used to use snuff in the eighteenth century."

"Yes, I remember you telling me that. It is a stunning ring."

"Yes," said Lady Elsmere. "It seems that you and I have fine taste when it comes to jewelry, Doreen."

Doreen relaxed and smiled. It seemed like Doreen loved flattery. If I had known that sooner, I would have really laid it on thick sooner.

"Doreen, you do look really wonderful considering the awful tragedy you're going through. How are you doing?" I said.

"I miss Addison terribly, but life must go on. And I have my daughter."

I nodded my head in agreement.

"Who would have thought that a simple aspirin would cause a person such harm?" said Lady Elsmere. "I keep thinking about how he got aspirin at my home, but can't come up with a clue. Charles, my butler, says he didn't ask for one. I just keep wondering. I so hope you're not going to hold that against me. It worries me so."

Doreen put her hands on Lady's Elsmere arm. "June, don't worry yourself about this. It was just an accident. Someone might have had a headache and put an aspirin in their drink and Addison picked up their glass by mistake."

"But no one claims to have used aspirin that night," I retorted.

Doreen gave me a sympathetic smile. "Of course, no one would admit to it. They don't want to be implicated in a man's death even if it was an accident. Afraid that I might sue or something like that. It's human nature to protect one's self."

"I'll drink to that," quipped Lady Elsmere, taking a swig out of the silver flask she had pulled from her purse. "You make me feel better about it, Doreen."

"It was just an accident, June. Unfortunate, but nothing more sinister that than. I don't harbor any resentment. None at all." Doreen looked around and saw a pathway through the throng of people. "Now, I must be going. I had no idea so many people would be here. It makes me nervous. Ta ta, ladies."

Lady Elsmere and I watched Doreen disappear hastily through the crowd.

Taking another swig out of her flask, Lady Elsmere swore, "She's guilty as hell. Snuff indeed."

"Her demeanor does give one pause. I don't think I would be so calm about someone putting aspirin in a drink and my husband dying by drinking from that glass. I certainly would want to know whose glass, even if it was an accident."

Meriah ran back and leaned over us. "What did she say?" whispered Meriah.

"We know for sure that her ring has a compartment, but we couldn't trip her up on anything else. She is unflappable," replied Lady Elsmere.

Meriah turned to me. "Well, it's up to you now to make it stick."

"Me?"

"You're the one with the police contacts. If anyone is going to convince the police to look into this further, it will have to be you," concluded Meriah.

"Yes, Josiah," joined in Lady Elsmere. "You will have to talk to Detective Goetz. You have a way with him and if anyone can get his attention, it's you."

"Jumping Jehosaphat!" I cried.

"What is it?" asked Meriah.

"I forgot to tell Doreen something important about Lacey Bridges," I said. "Oh well, the police will let her know, I'm sure."

Hearing a cough, I glanced at Jake. He was scowling at the three of us. He had been listening and did not like our investigating Addison's death. I knew that on the way home, he was going to read me the riot act.

But I was wrong.

Jake was quiet on the way home. That was because he was going to drop a bomb and was thinking of how to tell me.

I was also wrong about the police notifying Doreen that Lacey Bridges had been released.

I would have to live with the guilt of not telling her for the rest of my life.

20

I slept late. That's because I didn't get to bed until late. Rather I did get to bed, but I didn't get to sleep until the wee hours of the morning. Get my drift.

I was positively humming.

"Jake," I called, wrapping a filmy robe around me. "Jake."

"In here," answered Jake.

I went to his bedroom where I found him sitting on the bed staring out the patio door. I glanced at the bureau. It was empty of his possessions and his children's pictures were missing.

Slumping against the doorframe, I muttered, "Oh shit!"

Jake patted the mattress. Reluctantly I sat beside him. We sat quietly for a long time until he found the courage to speak. "I don't want to go but I have to. In fact, I've put this off as long as I could, but my children need me."

"For how long?"

Jake shrugged.

"I see." I played with the fringe on my robe. "May I ask why?"

"Pauline called. That's my ex-wife. She has cancer. I need go home and help with the children. Her mother has passed away and her sister lives in another state. There's only me."

"Is it terminal?" I asked, hoping. I know I'm awful at times.

"I hope not," answered Jake softly. "But I have to be there while she fights, so I'm going home to take care of things."

I placed my hand on his. His fingers tightened around mine.

"I understand, Jake."

"It's not that I won't . . . that I don't . . ."

"I love you, Jake."

"I've stocked the refrigerator and pantry. Mrs. Todd will be here tomorrow to help with the light cleaning and cooking. Charles is going to have the pastures mowed next week. All the bills are paid up for the month. Your medicine is in your bathroom with all the instructions."

"Even the pain medication?"

Jake chuckled as he touched my cheek. "Even the pain medication."

"Wow, you must really trust me."

"A new therapist will be here next Wednesday at nine a.m. He is going to give me a report, so you behave now."

"So everything is neat and tidy and tied with a ribbon. You have thought of everything and can leave knowing that life will continue without you."

"This is not what I wanted to happen. Please don't get angry."

"Will you call me, at least?"

"No."

"I know you think being blunt is kind, but it's not."

Jake gave my hand one last squeeze before rising from the bed. "Goodbye Josiah."

I tried not to notice the several tears running down my face.

Jake gave me one last look before walking out of the room. I sat on his bed until I heard the front door close.

I sat there until late afternoon shadows stretched across the floor. Then I got up and visited my honeybees. There in my beeyard, where thousands and thousands of honeybees flew around me, winging to their rhythm of life, I cried out my sorrow. And when I was finished, I knew that I would never cry over Jacob Dosh again.

BRANNON SAYS GOODBYE

I finally tracked Brannon down at Keeneland. A friend of mine had called and given me a tip that Brannon was there sitting in a box with some "swells."

Hurriedly I drove over to the prestigious racing course and parked my car. It took twenty-five minutes to locate him having a grand time, sipping champagne and exchanging jokes with people. Brannon always had told jokes well. That was one of the things I liked about him – he had always made me laugh, as he now did Ellen Boudreaux, who was hanging on his every word.

Not wanting to cause a scene, I wrote a note and paid a Keeneland attendant to hand it to Brannon. From the back, I watched Brannon read the note and then scan the bleachers. He leaned forward, saying something to Ellen, who smiled brightly at him.

My gawd – she was Asa's age. Her father donated to the UK Art Department and UK Art Museum. We had worked on exhibits together. What did he think of this September/May romance?

I hurried back to my old Mercedes. In a few moments, Brannon walked out into the parking lot and finding my car, got in. He did not seem pleased.

He just sat there, not saying anything.

"You said you were going to call," I accused.

Brannon looked out the window. "I wanted to spare you."

"Brannon, what's going on? I think I deserve some sort of answer."

"I want out, that's all. I don't want my old life."

"I'm so confused. When did all this start? Why didn't you tell me you were unhappy?"

"You knew, Josey. Don't pretend otherwise. It's just everything else took precedence – Asa's fiasco, the farm, your job – everything but me."

I was flabbergasted. Could he really be that self-centered and I not know it all these years? "I worked my tailbone off."

"As did I," he countered. "Now I'm tired and I want attention. I don't want to put up with those damn animals on the farm. I don't want the farm. The Butterfly – that's your achievement. It was never mine."

"What about Asa?"

"What about her? She's grown."

I gasped. "Brannon, she's your only child!"

For a moment, Brannon looked uncomfortable – as though he knew he had stepped over the line. "I didn't mean that." He looked towards me. "Really, I didn't. I just want to be free. I don't want to answer to any timetable. I'm tired, Josey. Can you understand that? I've reached a point in my life where all I want is pleasure." He wavered for a moment. "I don't know how else to explain it. I want pleasure."

"Come back home. We can work this out. I can resign from my job. We can travel to wherever you wish; do whatever you want."

Brannon shook his head. "Not going to work. I want my freedom."

"You want a divorce?"

"Jesus, Jo, what do you think I've been trying to convey to you? Yes, I want out, free and clear."

We were both silent for a long time. Finally I said, "There's the question of money. Bills still need to be paid that are in both our names. I should get part of your retirement fund especially since my father set you up in business."

"Can't. I'm broke. The firm's doing badly since Asa's mishap."

"You son of a bitch, blaming your cheapness on our daughter. I know for a fact that you were bought out. I talked to Wyman, Brannon. You were paid $500,000 for your share plus you raided all our accounts, leaving me with almost nothing. I also bet that you were given a severance package from work." I was mad now. Really mad.

"That money is mine."

"That money is ours. We both worked for it."

He sneered. "Good luck finding it. I'll just say I lost it at the track. That I have a gambling problem. The lawyers won't be able to trace it and neither will you."

I could hardly breathe. "When did you stop loving me, Brannon?"

"The day I started hating you."

21

"This better be good," huffed Detective Goetz as he entered my car parked in Jacobson Park.

I handed him a tuna sandwich and a bag of potato chips.

Goetz grunted after taking a bite. "Homemade." He took another large bite before taking a swig of his soft drink. "Haven't had homemade tuna salad in years. Real egg bits and celery. Good. Pickles too."

I ate some of my sandwich as well while observing Goetz. He had lost more weight since I had seen him last, which explained the new clothes plus a recent haircut. Concluding that he must be seeing someone, I put him on the "do not touch list."

"You know what today is?" I asked.

"Yeah. It is the one-year anniversary of the day you fell off the cliff. Is this what your call is about? Someone to commiserate with?"

"Goetz, don't get my nose out of joint after I just fed you. Can't you keep a lid on that mouth of yours for a few moments?"

"Sorry. Sometimes I understand why my wife left me. I'm a very good cop but a lousy partner for a woman. I just always say the wrong thing."

"Maybe women make you nervous."

"Just certain women," grinned Goetz. "We can talk about that night if you wish. Your recovery is quite remarkable. I never thought you'd walk again. Hell, I didn't think you were going to make it though the night. You were really beat-up."

"Actually I called you about another matter. To tell you the truth, I don't know why I brought up the anniversary."

"Because attention needs to be paid." He held up his soft drink. "I salute you. It's been a weird year for both of us and the crap hasn't settled yet."

Goetz and I sat staring over the dashboard of the car like two old battle-hard veterans mentally recounting the how and when that we received our wounds. We sat for the longest time until I spoke. "I think Doreen might have really killed Addison."

Goetz, who had been enjoying the silence, sighed. He was always sighing around me. "Why?"

I told him about the ring and showed him the picture of Dossi's portrait of Lucrezia Borgia. "She could have had ground up aspirin in the ring and easily spiked Addison's drink at the party."

Goetz pulled out his notebook. "I did some checking on Addison and came up with some interesting facts. Addison DeWitt was not English at all, but Italian. Everything was false about DeWitt: his accent, his background. He lied about everything. In fact he comes from a small population of Italians that are highly allergic to aspirin. It's a genetic condition."

"So just a little bit of aspirin would have pushed his system over the edge."

"That's what the geneticist told me," concurred Goetz.

"I wonder if Doreen knew."

"I went to talk to her about it. She says no, but she didn't seem all that shocked when I told her that DeWitt's real name was Gino Gimabotto. I'm not even sure that's not an alias."

"Criminal background?"

Goetz shook his head. "Naw. I just take him as a good looking boy with a certain way with the ladies who tried to make his way in the world by his looks and charm. He certainly hit the jackpot with Doreen. She took care of him. He didn't work."

"It sounds like you are open to suggestions that something like murder might have happened."

"It doesn't matter what I think. I can't prove it. The glasses and liquor showed nothing. Nobody witnessed anything amiss at the party. Except for Lacey Bridges' accusations, there was never any mention of a divorce, or that either Addison or Doreen were unhappy with each other. I talked to her neighbors and friends. Everyone says they were a devoted couple."

"But aren't you curious as to how the aspirin got into his system?"

"We know that he ingested it but that is all. It could have been as simple as residue from an aspirin that someone in the house took days before and didn't clean the glass properly. I don't think we'll ever know."

"So Doreen gets away with murder."

"I would go as far as saying that possibly his death might be suspicious, but murder is not provable."

"What if I could get you that ring?"

"No. She would have already cleaned the ring and you would just be getting yourself in trouble for nothing. You've got enough on your plate."

"Why do you say that?"

"I know that O'nan thinks he's going to get off."

"You've had contact with him?"

"He's working on a new angle. Trust me on this. He's gunning for you legally and that dope of a judge is falling for everything that creep says. O'nan is smart. He will stay away from you until the trial is over but he might have a good chance to walk. I'm just warning you. Make sure you and the DA are just as ruthless because O'nan has got something up his sleeve."

"Is there anything else you want to tell me?"

"Just be on the alert."

I could tell that Goetz knew more but he wasn't going to spill anything else to me. This was as far as he would go. Instinctively my hand touched my purse where I kept a stun gun. Maybe I should start carrying the handgun. Or maybe I should go ahead and tell Asa to have one of her minions whack O'nan. As far as morality was concerned, it went out the window when I woke up in the hospital a year ago. I'd rather be dead than go through such pain again. But then again, I rather that O'nan be dead.

And I didn't care who knew it.

22

Although the Revolutionary War had officially been over for ten months, it was still being fought in the frontier. In retaliation for a siege at Bryan Station in 1782, a group of militiamen under the leadership of John Todd of Fayette County followed a well-trained, battle-experienced British and Indian enemy force to Blue Licks, Kentucky. Daniel Boone, tagging along, warned that they were being led into an ambush.

Ignoring Boone's advice, a Captain McGary shouted, "Them that ain't cowards, follow me!"

The men, smelling blood, bravely followed Captain McGary. The only problem was the blood that they smelled was their own.

Witnesses recounted that Boone, in despair, said, "We are all slaughtered men."

Boone was right. The enemy force hid in ravines and surprised the frontiersmen, killing John Todd, an ancestor of Shaneika.

Fighting hand-to-hand combat, Boone, his son, Israel, and a handful of men were ordered to withdraw. Boone told his men to flee. Boone gave a captured horse to his son, Israel, but Israel refused to leave his father. Frantic, Boone tried to capture another horse only to see his son mortally shot in the neck. Boone escaped on horseback, leaving his dead son on the battlefield.

The Battle of Blue Licks was considered the worst defeat for Kentuckians of the war effort. Out of 176 men, 77 were killed and 11 captured. The battle lasted only fifteen minutes by some accounts.

In revenge, George Rogers Clark, brother of William Clark of the Lewis and Clark expedition to the Northwest, led a thousand men into Ohio and destroyed five Shawnee villages on the Great Miami River.

Four years later, the same foolish Hugh McGary, who had ignored Daniel Boone's warning and led those brave men to their death, asked the Shawnee chief, Moluntha, if he had been at Blue Licks. Moluntha had not been, but not really understanding the question, nodded yes.

Hugh McGary, in a rage, then took his tomahawk and killed Moluntha. McGary was court-martialed for murder, for murder it truly was.

And the bloodshed goes on and on . . . even in the quiet, tree-lined streets of today's Lexington.

I wasn't thinking of Kentucky's bloodied history, but I should have known that Kentucky was a beautiful siren who will have her way whether it is hard-living, battle-ready frontiersmen or a lovely woman on a day's outing. The black dirt of Kentucky will not be denied sacrifice. She must have her bones.

But the day was too beautiful even to care about such things. I was thinking of my bees.

It was time for wintering my hives. The leaves were starting to fall from the trees and if I waited much longer, it would be too late, as the temperature would fall below sixty degrees. Hives are not opened under sixty degrees.

Matt and one of Charles' grandsons worked the hives while I sat in my golf cart giving instructions. Meriah sat next to me admiring Matt's fortitude while she was covered head to toe in some getup to protect her from the bees.

All the honey supers had been stored in the barn, which left the hive boxes where the Queen and her workers lived. In order to protect them for winter, the top box is switched with the bottom box. As winter progresses the Queen will move up where extra food is stored. For some reason, Queens don't like to move down in their boxes.

"What are they doing now?" asked Meriah, her eyes bright as new copper pennies.

"They are putting pollen patties in the top of the hive so when the bees go to the top box, they will have more food in the winter. Some beekeepers do this. Some preach against it." I took a deep breath. "Matt is also putting in some Crisco patties with wintergreen oil. This helps keep pests away."

"Fascinating," replied Meriah.

"Honeybees are responsible for pollinating one-third of our food. Fruits, nuts and vegetables are the result of a honeybee's pollination. They even pollinate cotton for our clothes and bed sheets."

"I had no idea!" exclaimed Meriah. "I almost want to help Matt." She turned towards me, laughing, "But I won't."

I gave her a weak smile.

"What are those?"

"They are putting plastic inserts in the bottom of the hive to help the hive stay warm in the winter. Again, some beekeepers do this and some don't. I didn't do it one year and lost almost all my hives. It took three years to build the bees back up again."

Matt closed up the last hive and strode over to us.

"Did you get stung, honey?" asked Meriah.

Matt returned her cloying smile. "Just a few times. They seem in pretty good shape, Josiah. I'd say they've got at least sixty pounds or more honey stored in each hive."

I thought for a moment. "I'm going to feed them sugar water for a couple of days. I want to give them the best shot of getting through the winter as possible."

"Need help with that?"

I shook my head. "I've got a big rock where I put down food and they always find it."

Charles' grandson plopped in the back of the cart, causing it to rock. He gave me a cheeky grin.

Matt climbed in the back, too. "Home, James," he kidded.

I drove down the gravel driveway past the stable, which was full of horses from Lady Elsmere's farm boarding with us, while they built the new barn. I had checked my finances last night and it looked as though I was going to be in the black this year with the money from honey sales, the house tours and now the boarded horses. Some owners even talked about bringing their second string of horses here as they could easily traverse next door to use Lady Elsmere's training facility but board horses with me at a fraction of the cost. I was a very happy girl, indeed, that morning.

As I drove down the length of my farm, I was mentally calculating how much pasture I needed when Meriah screamed. I nearly drove off the road.

"Something's stung me," she cried.

"A bee probably ran into you accidentally," I responded, irritated that she was making such a big fuss. Hearing a gurgling sound, I turned. Meriah's face was turning red and she was clutching at her throat.

"Matt. Matt!" I cried. "I think Meriah's going into shock." I slammed on the brakes.

Matt jumped off from the back and came round to where Meriah was sitting.

"Meriah?" he asked. He looked at me with fright. "Where's your first aid kit?"

"Under the seat." I started to tear off Meriah's homemade get-up.

"WHERE?" cried Matt.

"Somewhere under the seat! Hurry, Matt. She's gagging."

Matt pushed Meriah's legs over and peered under them. "Found it." He threw the kit on the ground and rummaged around until he found an Epi-pen. Since he had used these on me due to my asthma, Matt knew exactly what to do. He thrust the pen to her thigh where he pushed down on the plunger. It immediately sent adrenalin into her system. Apparently Meriah was highly allergic to insect venom. Without adrenalin, she would be gone in minutes.

Meriah started to breathe again although somewhat raggedly. Matt jumped back in the cart as I raced towards the barn. There Matt jumped out and carried Meriah to Shaneika's car in front of the barn. I told Malcolm, Charles' grandson, to tell Shaneika what had happened and that we took her car as she always kept the keys in it at the farm. Within seconds, I was flying down Tates Creek Road with Matt holding Meriah in the back seat.

Malcolm had called the hospital and they were waiting for us at the emergency door with a gurney and a doctor. Matt followed Meriah inside while I went to park the car and tidy up. My hands where shaking as I looked for some rags or an old towel as Meriah had vomited in the back. I certainly did not want to return the car in its present state. I found a thin battered roll of paper towels and cleaned the back seat somewhat. Opening the back hatch, I began to look for a paper bag to put the towels in. In my haste to find something, I knocked over a small stained cardboard box of files. "Hell's Bells," I whispered under my breath. "I'm so clumsy."

Gathering the files, I tried to stack them and put them back in the box. That is when I saw a thick file with my daughter's name on it. Being me, I opened the file and read it.

Twenties minutes later, I was finished.

23

I waited for over an hour in the orange and yellow emergency waiting room before Matt came out and told me that he was staying at the hospital with Meriah until they released her. He would call Charles and have the Bentley sent over. "You look worn out," Matt said. "Go on home. I'll take care of this."

"Did she know she was allergic?"

"I don't think she had a clue. Meriah's never been stung before." Matt gave me a hug. "It could have been a wasp or even a sweat bee. It didn't have to be a honeybee. It probably got caught up in that garb she was wearing and trying to free itself. It's not your fault."

Reluctantly I left the hospital and, with my usual

dragging gait, found the SUV. There was a handwritten note on the windshield.

YOU'RE HELPING A MURDERER GO FREE!

I looked around but didn't see anyone suspicious. But I knew who had written it. Checking the tires and the gas tank, I just hoped Lacey hadn't crawled under the car and cut the brake line. I drove carefully out of the parking lot testing the brakes before heading for the police station. There I found Goetz slumped over a nasty-looking metal desk eating a garlic bagel from Blue Moon Farm with cream cheese.

"She's becoming a pest," I declared, throwing the note on his desk.

"I'll call Lacey's shrink. She is court ordered to see a therapist on a regular basis at that hospital complex."

"I bet she was going to an appointment when she saw me in the parking lot."

"No doubt. I don't think she's following you."

"I hope you called Doreen and let her know that Lacey is out."

"I left a message for her to call me but she hasn't yet."

"You better go by Doreen's house if she doesn't return your call."

"Why do you care? You think Doreen is guilty of murder."

"If she is, then she deserves her day in court . . . not to be hounded by some lunatic."

"Simpatico?"

"Maybe. Are you going to give me some of that bagel?"

Goetz hunched over his desk protecting his bagel from my grasp. "Go buy your own."

"I will next Saturday at the Farmers' Market. Selfish," I accused, before storming out of his office. What does it say about a man who won't share a garlic bagel?

I had one more thing to do before I called it a day. Heading back to my place, I stopped in at the barn. A barn hand told me that Shaneika had taken my golf cart and was waiting for me at the Butterfly. It only took several minutes more to reach home. The front door was wide open. Great.

Walking into the Butterfly, all the doors and windows were open. A record playing on my old console was blaring. Hearing me come in, Baby raced to greet me, and after nudging my hand for a pet, ran back out to the patio in sheer ecstasy.

In the pool was Shaneika in one of my bathing suits, sitting upright on a float sipping a martini. She waved to me.

"I guess my safety means nothing to you."

Shaneika whipped off her sunglasses. "There is no one after little-old-you right now. Quit living like a hermit and open this house up. It needs to breathe." She kept muttering, "Everything has to be locked up. Two alarm systems. Cameras all over the farm. Gee, you'd think you were someone important like the President."

I reached down and flipped the float over.

Shaneika came up coughing, "Hey, what's the matter with you?"

Throwing a towel at her, I said, "I need to see you as soon as you're dressed." With that I began the process of locking up the house again as well as turning on the cameras and rebooting the alarm systems. Once everything was back in place, I made myself some tea.

Forty-five minutes later, Shaneika showed up in the kitchen. "I'm sorry. I didn't think I'd put your nose out of joint by using the pool."

"You didn't . . . with that."

"Then what?"

I threw Asa's file across the counter.

Shaneika's eyes grew wide at the sight of it.

"Well?"

"I can explain."

"Then do."

"It was at Asa's request."

"Why would Asa want you to keep a file on her?"

Shaneika hesitated.

"If you don't tell me, I'll call Asa."

Shaneika sang like a bird. "It just was easier to get information on Asa from agencies if I accessed the info myself. Asa wanted to find out what information was out there about her. It was her way of keeping tabs on what was documented without actually being involved. Each time she comes into town, she asks for the file."

"Now why would you do that for my daughter?"

"Remember when I first met you, I said that I owed Asa a favor."

I nodded.

Shaneika took a deep breath. "When I passed the bar, I went to work for a big pharmaceutical company in New Jersey, which had been aggressively recruiting minorities. It was a respected company even though it farmed out the actual making of the drugs to China. After several years with the company, my security clearance was given a higher status, so I was getting some classified memos. But it was really by chance that I came across email memos stating that the company knew that the new diet pill they were perfecting caused cell anomalies in the gut."

"In other words, intestinal cancer."

"There was enough to suggest there was a possibility that long-term use of this drug might cause cancer, but so do a lot of other drugs. That was not the problem. Just more testing needed to be done.

"What was alarming was that the company was covering the data up and not willing to do more research. They just wanted FDA approval and to move the drug on to the market as soon as possible. Although I had no proof, I strongly suspected that FDA officials were being bribed to ramrod this drug through."

"So?"

"I couldn't live with that. I had met Asa during law school at UK. She was an undergraduate then, but was already taking advanced courses. Asa stood out and we gradually began an acquaintance, saying hi at the cafeteria or at the library. She was impressive even at that young age and through the years I kept up with her. When I made my decision to go public with the emails, I contacted her company for help. It was due to Asa's help that the information went public, but I was never caught as the whistle blower. After the furor at the company died down, I resigned and came back to Kentucky, but I never suffered any consequences. Without Asa's help, I probably would have lost my savings, been barred from practicing law and banned from working for other companies. I owed her a lot and still do."

"Much of the information in her file is wrong."

"We know that. We are just keeping tabs on what others are saying about her. Lots of influential people don't want Asa to resurface, but Asa is becoming powerful again in certain circles. She's gaining overseas contacts. That worries a lot of enemies so they put out misinformation."

"I'll use the real word for it – lies." I believed Shaneika but I would have to verify her story with Asa. Anyway I said, "Please put that in a better hiding place."

Shaneika nodded like a scolded child and tucked the file under her arm.

"Tell me something. Does my daughter frighten you?"

"I would say that I find the need for caution. I make sure that I never lie to her."

"Do you think she is a sociopath?"

Shaneika thought for a moment. "She has a very rigid moral code. There are no greys for her. There are good people and bad people. In that way, she is very simplistic, sort of like a female Dirty Harry and like Dirty Harry, Asa makes practical choices and acts on them. She thinks some people are just taking up space." Shaneika looked at me with concern. "Just because Asa gets her hands dirty from time to time doesn't mean that she is dirty herself. It's just how you have to play the game."

I took a sip of my tea. "I read the psych evaluation in the file. It was disturbing."

"That was the prosecution's psychiatrist. Yes, Asa will bend the rules to get things done. That doesn't make her crazy. It makes her effective. Most people don't like that because they can't control her. After Asa got framed, that little innocent Southern girl died and something else took her place."

"The defense evaluation wasn't much better, just couched in better terms." I took another sip of my tea. "When Asa was a child, she was very good with animals, so kind and gentle with them, but with other children her age . . . I had to keep an eye on her. She liked to dominate her playmates, bend them to her will. I guess in ancient times that need to dominate would have been seen as a maker of kings, but I always found it troublesome. The only people she was ever close to besides her father and me was her high school boyfriend whom she dumped right after high school graduation."

For once Shaneika said nothing but shifted her feet.

"Do you know anything about her personal life?"

"No."

"Nothing?"

"I think she works all the time."

"You wouldn't be fibbing to me, would you, Shaneika?"

"I've never lied to you, Josiah. Never."

I gave her the motherly "I'll know if you do lie" look before cutting her loose. "I don't mind you using the pool anytime. Just don't cut off my security protocol. You may feel strong and safe, but I don't."

"I think I better go."

"One more thing, Shaneika. Do you trust Asa?"

Shaneika didn't hesitate. "With my life."

"Okay then. Yes, I hear your mother calling for you." That was my little code line that meant go home. It was the first time since I had known Shaneika that she had deferred to me. I liked it.

"Shaneika," I said as she was leaving.

"Yeah?"

"Thanks for being here for Asa and me. I won't forget it."

Giving a dimpled smile, Shaneika replied, "We girls gotta stick together. The world can be awfully cold." Then she clattered down the hallway in her crocs and out to her black SUV, forgetting to close the front door.

So much for my security talk.

24

Sitting with a legal notepad on my lap, I wrote down reasons why I thought Doreen had murdered Addison.

Motive – Money

Opportunity – Matt's engagement party

How – Drugging his bourbon with ground-up aspirin

Method of delivery – A poison ring just like Lucrezia Borgia's

I looked up aspirin poisoning on the computer and was shocked at what I found.

Every year, the use of NSAIDs (Non-Steroidal Anti-Inflammatory Drugs) accounts for an estimated 7,600 deaths and 76,000 hospitalizations in the United States. NSAIDs include aspirin, ibuprofen and some stuff I had never heard of like tiaprofenic acid, diclofenac, ketoprofen and naproxen. It was also highly suspected that the overdosing of aspirin during the 1918 Influenza pandemic caused many deaths attributed to the flu.

I had always thought aspirin was a wonder drug with no side effects. Apparently for many, it really was highly toxic. Hmmm.

Yet in the correct dosage, aspirin saves millions from heart attacks and strokes.

I kept writing on my pad.

Witnesses – Lots, but no one understood what they saw.

When drug was administered – Must have been right before Jake and I arrived. It seemed the most likely conclusion is that Addison ingested the deadly drink at the toast or right after.

Maybe it was time for me to go nosing around the people who had arrived before I did. I called June.

"You want me to invite all the women for a bridal shower? That's awfully short notice, Josiah!" exclaimed Lady Elsmere.

"Every woman that was there except for Doreen."

"Won't that look suspicious?"

"Who cares? We'll use the excuse to gather everyone for a bridal shower. If there are questions about Doreen not being invited . . . we will just say that you thought she was still in mourning. I'm sure you can come up with a good reason."

"You mean I take the blame."

"That's right. For once take some responsibility."

June snorted into the phone and hung up.

Smiling, I put down the phone. I knew she would do it.

Two days later I was in the Lady Elsmere's drawing room holding a gaudily wrapped bridal gift for Meriah who was ooohing and ahhing while opening assorted colorful packages brought by bored women who were glad for a chance to get out of their houses . . . or rather away from their demanding children and disinterested husbands.

Meriah puckered up her orange lips, air kissing some matron who had given her a Cuisinart. "I just looooove it," she schmoozed.

I snickered. I doubted that Meriah's dainty fingers would ever touch the controls of the expensive machine, but maybe her Hispanic cook's would. Sensing the cause of my snicker, Meriah narrowed her eyes at me.

I batted my eyes back at her.

"Has anyone heard how Doreen is doing?" asked Ginger Konkler, who looked like an overgrown hobbit complete with broad glowing cheeks and twinkling button eyes. She had the nasty habit of grinning all the time and being so cheerful I just wanted to tweak her nose . . . really hard. "I'm surprised she isn't here."

Lady Elsmere said without missing a beat, "Yes, I'm surprised she isn't here as well."

"Why didn't she come?" asked Sally Durham, a former Kentucky beauty queen twenty years past, but still perky, tits and all.

God, I hated her.

"More tea?" asked Lady Elsmere, reaching for perky Sally's teacup.

172

"I still can't get over Addison's death," I stated, wanting to get this show on the road.

"Terrible, terrible," all the ladies murmured in unison.

"I just don't know how Addison got hold of that aspirin. Did anyone see anything?"

All the ladies clucked and turned to each other in a sympathetic chorus, "No, I didn't. Neither did I. Can't imagine."

That is, all except Beryl Hubble, who stared at the plate balancing on her very large kneecap with her meaty face a nice shade of pink. She blew a wad of carbon dioxide out of her mouth, looking very much like a blowfish.

Our eyes caught when she arched her Joan Crawford eyebrows only to have her peepers slide back down towards her lap.

Bulls-eye!!!!

Meriah took up her cue to poke and pry the herd, with Lady Elsmere coming behind to round the ladies up verbally, but to no avail. Nobody had seen anything untoward.

I was just waiting for an opportunity with Beryl. She knew something. I could feel it.

After several women had visited the powder room, Beryl excused herself as well. This was my opportunity. I waited several minutes and then followed Beryl. I went right in as the front part of the powder room had a two-sink counter, with the toilet in an adjoining room. Beryl was dabbing her face with a damp hand towel.

"Oh sorry, Beryl. Didn't mean to disturb you. Just want to check my hair." I went over and stood next to her. We both looked like sad sacks if you asked me.

Beryl averted her eyes.

I could see she was a scared little rabbit and it was up to me to shake her from the bramble bush.

"Beryl, did you see something the night of the engagement party?"

Beryl's eyes widened. The look reminded me of Janet Leigh's when she turned around and found someone invading her nice hot shower with a butcher knife. You know the movie.

"Beryl?"

"NO!"

"I think you did."

"I don't want to get involved."

"Even if it might be murder? You're some good citizen."

"You're not going to bully me, Josiah. My son just finished medical school. He's going to Johns Hopkins for his residency. I'm not going to tarnish his reputation with something as sullying as a murder."

I had to admire her guts in standing up to me, but that would not keep me from going for her throat. "Beryl, if you don't tell me what you know, I'm going to tell everyone about that affair you had with your son's married soccer coach and that you used to do the nasty with him in the parking lot of the Parkette."

"I knew I should never have confided in you." She pointed a finger at me. "You swore to secrecy."

"And I've told no one all these years, but this is murder, Beryl."

After blinking her eyes, dabbing her nose and sighing, Beryl came clean.

"It's probably nothing but I was standing next to Doreen and Addison during the toast. They both were drinking Kentucky bourbon, but she gave Addison her glass to hold so she could drink the champagne that Charles was handing out. Then I came into this very powder room on the night of the engagement just seconds after the official toast was given."

"Yeah?"

Beryl leaned forward whispering. "Doreen was in here rinsing out a bourbon glass."

"You saw her rinse out a glass?"

Beryl thought for a moment. "I saw her pour water out of a bourbon glass into the sink."

"How do you know it wasn't white wine?"

"It was water, I'm sure. Wine has a different look to it from water. I'm sure it was water. And Doreen looked startled. I mean she jumped a little bit when I came in."

"Did you ask her what she was doing?"

"No. I thought she just didn't like the taste of her drink and was rinsing out the glass."

"Why wouldn't she just place the glass on a piece of furniture or hand it to Charles, if she didn't like it?"

"I don't know," whined Beryl. "People have their own patterns of doing things and maybe that was hers. I didn't think it was a big deal at the time."

"But you did later?"

"Not too long after Addison had his fit. Josiah, you're not the only one with a quick mind around here. I just felt something was suspicious."

"And because you're the wife of a doctor and the mother of a doctor, you know when something looks wrong."

"I just felt something was off – I had a bad case of the . . . of the . . . "

"The 'icks'?"

"That word will do nicely. Yes, I felt icky. I don't know why."

"So you're the one who called the police."

Beryl gave a nice little smile. "I called from the phone in the upstairs bedroom and wouldn't give my name. Just said someone had died and the police had better come."

"Why didn't you tell the police what you saw?"

"Because it meant nothing at the time. I just had a feeling. But when word got around that Addison had died from aspirin poisoning, it began to prey on my mind. I guess it was her reaction to me coming in that was so puzzling. She really looked startled."

"Why didn't you tell anyone then?"

"I told you why." Beryl stamped her foot. "I don't want to get involved."

"But you have a theory, Beryl."

She gave me another shy smile.

"Come on – spill."

"I've been thinking hard on this, Josiah. Let's say that Doreen really gave aspirin to Addison. Here's how I think she did it.

"She puts the aspirin in her own bourbon drink and then hands it to Addison to hold during the toast. Then after the toast, she retrieves his glass of bourbon. Addison either doesn't notice that she took his glass or doesn't care – after all, they are married and married couples share plates and glasses all the time, even toothbrushes. Addison takes a few sips and suffers an allergic reaction minutes later."

"Brilliant deduction."

"Josiah, if you breathe a word of this to anyone, I will simply deny it. I will tell people that you made it up for your own amusement. You can't afford to get mixed up either, with all these rumors that Asa stole into Ellen Boudreaux's house."

"That's a lie."

Beryl gave me a sly look. "Everyone believes she did. Asa was always a strange one, even when a child. So precocious. So aloof. I was always glad that she was too old to play with my son."

I don't know what happened but my wolf head cane shot out and rapped Beryl on the ankle. I was so shocked that I couldn't utter any apology. Instead I went back to the shower, taking my seat.

A few minutes later, Beryl walked, or rather limped, back nursing a swelling ankle.

Meriah gave her a curious look.

"What happened to you?" asked Lady Elsmere, ringing for Charles.

"Nothing," murmured Beryl. "I think I twisted my ankle."

"My goodness. That's too bad," we all clucked in unison.

"Yes Madam?" asked Charles upon entering the room.

"Miss Beryl seems to have injured her ankle. Can you bring her an ice pack and some aspirin?"

"NO ASPIRIN!" we all shouted at Charles.

Nonplussed, Charles asked, "Will Tylenol do, ma'am?"

We all looked at Beryl, who suddenly liked being the center of attention. "No, not even that, Charles. How about a stiff whiskey and a ride home?"

"Very good, ma'am. That we can accommodate."

The shower ended an hour later – with a soused Beryl having the flexibility of Jell-O and a bag of mushy peas taped around her ankle, being helped into the Bentley. She was also wearing Lady Elsmere's new garnet and diamond sunburst brooch, which was a little inducement not to sue me.

As far as I saw the afternoon, it was a win-win situation for everyone, including Beryl.

June didn't need that brooch anyway. She had plenty of little doodads that sparkled.

25

I entered the Curl Up and Dye Beauty Shop on upper Limestone with some trepidation. I wondered about the name.

Everyone turned and looked at me. Gave me a real good look before returning to their business.

A pretty lady with intelligent dark eyes strode over to me, with the nametag of Tamara on her shift. "Are you Mrs. Reynolds?"

"Yes."

"Have a seat. I'm a little behind, but will be with you shortly."

I took a seat and peered at outdated copies of Ebony magazine and waited and waited and waited . . . and waited. Forty-five minutes later, I was led to her station.

"That was a long wait," I complained.

Ignoring my complaint, she started feeling my hair. "Now what can I do for you? Your hair feels a little dry to me."

"Doreen DeWitt recommended you. She said you gave the best cuts in town."

The beautician gave a quick smile.

"Oh yes, Miss Doreen has been my customer for several years. That's nice that she referred you." She swung my chair around to face her. "Let's get you shampooed."

She was one of the few hairdressers that still gave a head massage when washing hair. I was simply purring when sitting back at her station.

Doreen had learned of the bridal shower and had called June, raising cain about being left out. To make amends, Meriah took Doreen out to lunch while I made a beeline to Doreen's house to question her staff. That was three days ago.

I wasn't thinking at all of the fifty bucks I'd bribed Doreen's housekeeper to tell me the name of her hairdresser. It seemed to me that a person would confess to their priest or if they were protestant . . . to a therapist, bartender or hairdresser. Many women told their hairdressers the most appalling secrets. Since Doreen wasn't Catholic and her housekeeper said she wasn't seeing a therapist, I took the last one, hoping to hit the jackpot.

Boing!

"Wasn't it terrible about Doreen's husband dying suddenly like that," I commented as my hair was being combed out.

"It sure was. Just terrible."

"He was so young."

"Sure was." Snip. Snip. Cut. Cut. Comb out. Snip. Snip again.

"She was devastated by Addison's death. She loved him so."

The hairdresser twisted her mouth but said nothing. Snip. Snip.

Boing!

"Well, didn't she?"

"I'm not one to tell tales."

That's no good.

I tried a different tack. "She did confide in me one time that they were having trouble."

She nodded her head while cutting. "Not so much having trouble as being bored."

"That's right. She said she was bored."

She quit cutting my hair and looked in the mirror at me. "I remember her saying that a wet dish rag was more interesting." She laughed. It sounded like cool water trickling down a moss-covered cliff in the forest.

"And that she was going to divorce him?"

"Get rid of him, anyway."

"Get rid of him?"

" Unnhnn. That's exactly what she said – get rid of him. Now don't you go tell her that I spilled the beans. It's just that everything worked out fine."

Boing!

"At least it did for her."

"Whatcha mean?"

"It didn't work so well for Addison DeWitt."

Tamara waved the scissors around. "The Lord made that decision to take Mr. DeWitt. No one can fault the Lord. Mr. DeWitt's in heaven, happy as a clam with his Savior."

She went on cutting my hair.

But what if Tamara was wrong and Doreen had decided to play God. I wondered about Addison being happy with his Savior then.

26

"I did talk to them," yelled Goetz. "Quit bugging me on this. In fact, I told you not to pursue this. I said unless information just happened to come your way."

I threw a sandwich at him. We were sitting again in my car watching kids fly kites in Jacobson Park.

He opened it up in a hurry and reached in my basket to see if there were chips.

Taking a bite, he moaned. "Old fashioned egg-salad sandwich. I haven't had one in years. My mother used to make these for me. Let me see. Let me see," he said smacking his lips. "A little more tart than hers but good . . . really good."

"What did they say?" I asked, nudging him. Goetz took out his worn out notebook, flipping it open. "Miss Beryl says and I quote, 'Josiah Reynolds is a god-damned liar.' She also said that you attacked her with your cane and wants to press charges."

"Then she has to give the brooch back."

"What's that?"

"Nothing."

"You can count her out for backing up your story. She wouldn't pee on you if you were on fire."

"Thanks for that analogy."

"I really love that you added onions to the mix. It gives a little more kick. My mother never did that."

"Probably because you were a child. She might have added a little sugar."

"Never thought of that." He took another bite, finishing his sandwich. Immediately his big hairy bear claw of a hand was rooting around in my basket. Thank goodness I had brought plenty of sandwiches. This man could really eat when he set his mind to it.

"Go on," I encouraged. "What about Tamara?"

"This gets even better. She says she doesn't remember what you two talked about except that you said that Doreen DeWitt referred you. I don't know why but I have a sinking feeling if I were to ask Mrs. DeWitt that – she might deny it."

"Doesn't it strike you odd that a rich white woman would go to a beauty shop on the other side of town?"

"Nope."

"Women like her go to salons on the south side of town."

Goetz stopped chewing for a moment and then swallowed. "Speaking of that, your hair looks real nice."

I continued. "She went there because she's cheap and because she could talk about her feelings without any of her peers going to the same shop. No possibility for gossip. Everyone has to have an outlet to vent, even Doreen."

"Your hair doesn't look as dry."

"Tamara told me that Doreen said that she was going to get rid of Addison – not divorce, but get rid of."

"Hearsay."

"Come on now."

"I think you should go back to Tamara. She did a great job on your hair. Really looks good."

I slapped his hand when he reached for another sandwich.

"You should do something about that temper of yours. Red hair shouldn't mean that women have to be fierce."

"It's the Viking blood. It never really gets bred out."

"Keep this up and it's going to be an anger-management program for you, girlie."

"So Doreen will get away with murder."

"Maybe. We don't know for sure that a murder took place. It's all conjecture. No hard evidence."

"Learn to live with it?"

"Why not?" answered Goetz with a disgusted snarl. "I've had to live with crappier things. So have you." He got out of the car, slamming the door.

So that was that.

27

Days later, I reluctantly dragged myself out of bed. It was a crisp, golden fall day, but I didn't care. Somehow I got dressed and drove my little golf cart over to June's. The house was a beehive of activity as the wedding reception was to take place there after the ceremony.

Not wanting to get in the way, I turned the cart around and checked on my hives. The bees were active and flew through the cart. A few settled on me, culling the golden-rod pollen from their bodies onto the pollen baskets on the backs of their legs. Then they too flew off.

I kept thinking of Doreen and Addison. There seems to be no end to our evil ways in Kentucky, which was just as Chief Dragging Canoe had warned Old Daniel. It is a land under a cloud and a dark and bloody ground.

186

On another beautiful fall day in 1941, Marion Miley, a nationally known athlete, who beat Babe Didriksen at the 1937 Augusta Invitational, was with her mother at the Lexington Country Club on Paris Pike. Two trashy men, masked, brandishing guns and up to no good, surprised them. Moments later, twenty-seven year old Marion Miley lay dead on the floor of the prestigious Lexington Country Club. Her mother, gravely injured, crawled for help.

Being young, strong and famous didn't save Miss Marion – just like being handsome, strong and admired didn't save Addison DeWitt.

I don't know why I was thinking of Marion Miley, except that it was another useless killing of a vital young person in the Bluegrass.

It gave me a headache to think of them, Marion and Addison, but I couldn't get those two out of my mind. Time passed and I must have fallen asleep, as I awoke after being stung. "Jumping Jehosaphat," I muttered, pulling the stinger out of my hand. I must have twitched the wrong way in my sleep. The sun was still warm on my face and now there were hundreds of bees exploring. Starting the cart, I made my way to the Butterfly. Bees flew out as soon as they felt the rumble of the vehicle and others, more stalwart, clung on. I parked the cart. Sooner or later the remaining bees would make their way home to their hives.

Feeling drab, I must have made a sorry sight unlocking the door to the Butterfly. She needed a better mistress.

Checking the clock, I had just enough time to get dressed and make it to the church.

In the end I was late as usual. After parking, I made my way quietly into the small limestone church. Meriah was walking down the aisle.

I winced, knowing that Matt would be furious with me for being late. Seeing me come in and take a place in the back, Matt gave a slight nod.

I had to admit it.

Meriah was beautiful.

Her dress was beautiful.

Matt was beautiful.

And the church was beautiful with its liberal use of white roses and lilies, which played well against the grey limestone walls.

Lady Elsmere was up front standing with Charles and his wife.

I smiled.

June always liked to be up where the action was. The mayor was standing behind her, as were some very famous mystery and horror writers who were friends of Meriah's. There were several TV stars and many local celebrities dotted here and there. And there was Doreen sitting only a few pews ahead of me. She was wearing a frothy pink hat with little dyed pink feathers, which seemed out of kilter with the time of the year. The hat should have been a fall color as the trees were losing their coverage and the ground was brilliant in full autumn colors of crisp leaves.

Meriah looked radiant as she faced Matt.

Matt was trembling, but gave a brave smile.

Reverend Humble gave us permission to sit, for which I was extremely thankful. Matt wasn't the only one trembling.

I didn't pay much attention after that. I was drowning in my own thoughts of how everyone was leaving. I would have to start my life anew and somehow find purpose again. It would be another major struggle. I was wondering if I had the courage to face it when I recognized that vows were being spoken. I heard Meriah say "I do" and then Reverend Humble mumbled something to Matt. A few seconds of silence. Then I heard the Reverend repeat Matt's vows and then Meriah saying, "Matt?"

A door opened and closed. Curiously, I turned to see who else was late and was astonished to see Lacey Bridges standing behind me, searching the assembled. What was she doing?

Lacey's eyes lightened on someone.

There wasn't much time to wonder what she was up to before she pulled something out of a clutch bag and strode past to where Doreen sat.

Before anyone could react, Lacey leaned over several people and pointed a gun at Doreen, pulling the trigger.

BANG! BANG!

The shots rang out and reverberated throughout the small stone chapel.

Everyone screamed, including myself.

Panic ensued with people throwing themselves on the stone floor or jumping over the cushioned pews trying to make their way out. Stunned, I couldn't move while watching as the world collapsed around me in utter confusion. Matt pulled Meriah with him through a side door without giving me a glance. Even those sitting next to Doreen had scurried out from underneath the pews and made it to safety.

Doreen slumped in the pew while Lacey screamed curse words at her. The pink hat now looked very sad, sitting lopsided on her head – the part that had not been blown off.

Slowly looking down, I noticed there was blood on my beige suit and feebly tried to wipe it off. There was debris on my face, which fell into my lap. Realizing that the debris was tiny bits of brain, I frantically tried to shake them off.

That's when Lacey noticed me still sitting in the back pew.

Oh merde!

Lacey looked as shocked as anyone. "I had to do it. I told you that she was guilty and she was going to get away with it." She began laughing. "She's done for now. No way was I going to let Doreen get away with killing my Addison. No way." She wiggled the gun in my direction. "You do believe me, don't you, Mrs. Reynolds? That I had to do it?"

I nodded.

Lacey smiled sweetly and then put the gun in her mouth.

I shut my eyes.

Epilogue

Fumbling in my wallet, I finally found the key to Asa's New York apartment. I gave the door a good shove and reached inside to find the light. I gave a finn to the young man helping me with my luggage and thanked him before shutting the door. He said I reminded him of his grandmother.

Hmmm.

I found the alarm keypad and punched in the numbers Asa had given me.

Beep.

With that task done, I went through the door, looking around while talking off my coat. The apartment was sparsely furnished. There was a couch, two chairs, some end tables and that's it. No flowers, no plants, no knickknacks, no pictures, no books. It looked like a hotel room. The living room opened up to a balcony from which sprang a fantastic view of the city. I opened the balcony doors, letting in the evening air.

Going back inside I turned on the rest of the lights. It was then I saw it. Catching my breath, I had to sit down. Like an idiot I just sat staring at it with my mouth open.

There above the fireplace hung the Duveneck painting, the one I had given to Brannon for our wedding anniversary and he then gave to his girlfriend. It had cost me an entire year's salary. Around the painting was a new frame – sterling . . . with a note attached to it.

I plucked the ivory envelope from the frame and opened it with shaking hands.

Dear Mother,

Here is the return of your painting that is rightfully yours. Due to its provenance, I think it best we keep it here. The frame is covered from silver melted from the jewelry Dad took that awful evening when he left us. I figure things are pretty even now. Happy belated Mother's Day. Love always, Asa.

I smiled while tearing up the note.

Exciting Bonus Chapter

<u>Death by Lotto</u>

Prologue

Ethel Bradley had fallen asleep in front of the flickering TV. It was too bad. If she had been awake, she might have discovered that she had won the lotto jackpot. The numbers that she played every week – the birthdays of her deceased husband and son – for over seventeen years, had finally come in.

The lotto ticket was safely tucked inside her fist, which rested upon her heaving lap. A hand gently reached over and pulled the ticket from her hand while the announcer re-read the numbers.

Stunned at winning, the hand returned the ticket to its owner's lap. This would have to be done with care, thought the person to whom the hand belonged.

Everyone knew Ethel played those same numbers every week.

There was no way the ticket could be stolen and the world not know about it. This would have to be thought through very carefully. But one thing was for sure. There was no way Ethel Bradley was going to enjoy one dollar from that winning lotto ticket.

No damn way in hell!

CPSIA information can be obtained
at www.ICGtesting.com
Printed in the USA
FFOW031212080413
1078FF